# THE
# SIGNAL

## REBECCA S.W. BATES

D.M. Kreg Publishing
DMKregPublishing.com

In loving memory of my dad, who showed me the stars from Brazil.

# Acknowledgments

Thanks to the many writers who helped this project during its early stages: the Boulder Lunch Bunch, who helped me launch the idea; the Northern Colorado Writers Workshop, who endured endless early drafts. Special thanks go to the Inklings, who helped me visualize the final draft, and to my first readers, Al and Emily, who rearranged their schedules to accommodate mine. Thanks also to Donald Kreg, editor and publisher extraordinaire.

# Chapter One

LANDON WALKER GRIPPED THE HANDHOLDS so tightly that his knuckles ached. Peering through the viewport of SpaceHab's weightless hub, he watched the court-ordered shuttle drift away from the wheel, toward the shimmering, blue sphere of Earth, a mere 35,000 kilometers away. It took a large part of his life with it, leaving behind...

Nothing but silence.

It was better this way. Better for everyone. For the baby. For his work. Still, someone else — the courts, not him — had decided to remove her, and that's what really gnawed at him. His own flesh and blood was as much out of his control as the rest of his life.

The sleek spaceplane reflected the Sun on its shiny siding, dwindling to a spark of light, then a flicker. And finally, nothing. Walker squinted hard at the empty spot where he'd last glimpsed the shuttle.

Gone. Everything that had ever really mattered...gone. He was spiraling toward a dead-end after all the promise he'd shown, the excitement he'd generated back at Port Lowell with his initial research.

"Dr. Walker?" An apologetic voice from behind disturbed his thoughts.

Walker stiffened. No one ever saw him with a slump to his spine. He hated feeling sorry for himself. He glanced over his shoulder and saw one of the young technicians from his lab. "Yes, what is it?"

The tech cringed slightly as if he'd caught a whiff of Walker's stale breath. "Excuse me, sir, but we thought you'd want to know right away." His face flushed, and he looked away.

Walker released the handhold and whisked fingers across his chin, badly in need of a shave. He straightened the belt of his khaki jumpsuit, rumpled from having slept in it. Upright, all night, beside the crib. Waiting for an opportunity to hold her, never certain how to hold anyone so little. So needy.

"Go ahead," Walker urged, turning around to give the tech his full attention.

"It's the lab, sir. Seems we've picked up an emission coming from the direction of Alpha Centauri."

"Uh-huh," Walker said, allowing only his cool exterior to show, while inside he wanted to explode. Just one kind of emission interested him. He swallowed hard. "What kind?"

"Tachyonic."

Walker whistled softly. "Anyone else report it? Port Lowell? Lunar Observatory? Van Pelt's group?"

"Not yet, sir."

"Damn," Walker muttered.

The kid's brow lifted, and Walker turned away from him, glanced once more at the empty spot on the viewport. "Let's go," he said finally, pushing off through weightlessness toward the tube leading to his laboratory. "We've got work to do."

———

LIEUTENANT CHICO TORRES eyed the shapely curves of the civilian passenger strapped into his co-pilot's seat. "Ready, ma'am?" He snapped his visor into place for the short hop over to Valles Marineris — the grandest canyon of the solar system, and it happened to be here on Mars.

The boss-lady administrator from personnel hesitated a fraction of a second too long to suit him. "Chico, I really appreciate your doing this on your time off. Especially on such short notice. I owe you one."

*You sure as hell do, babe.* But what he said was, "Forget it, ma'am. It's nothing." He couldn't afford to fuck up. Not now.

The slight vibration of the hydraulic system tickled through his spine and lifted the Thin Air Skimmer — this newest model of the TASK flyer — up from the warrens of base toward the bay door on the surface of Mars. Despite its name, Port Lowell did not face openly onto the sea of space where ships could freely come and go. It burrowed, instead, under the regolith, which was just a fancy word for dirt. All the same, it left Chico feeling smothered.

He wondered how his passenger had bent regulations for her impromptu holiday. Did her boyfriend know that she was about to join him over at the construction site? That was her business, and it was his business to make Ms. Administration happy.

The lift system clanked into place, nesting the cockpit of the two-person skimmer against sealed doors. They waited while air emptied into holding tanks, then the bay doors slid open. Glancing once more at his passenger, he waited for a last-minute change of her capricious mind. But it didn't come. She stared intently at the dark landscape ahead.

He followed her gaze. Nothing had changed. The backdrop still showed the cone outline of Olympus Mons sprawling above an otherwise empty horizon like a giant tit. A place like this made the plains of his Colorado homeland seem downright lush.

"TASK 411, you are cleared for exit."

"Roger." He looked again at his passenger. She nodded, and he set the controls to automatic. A gentle thrust rippled through the craft, then they slipped off the pad into a pre-dawn sky. The green read-out in his contact lens scrolled through numbers that matched their altitude.

He felt his heart soar as the skimmer lifted up into the chilly, thin atmosphere. This was what he was born to do. He'd known it as long ago as his twelfth birthday, when he'd built his first hang glider all by himself, then jumped off the butte near town. He could still hear the *abuelita*, his mother's mother, screech at him. "You want to kill me with your death, Chiquito?"

He pushed her voice and everything else from his mind as he concentrated on the flyer's union with the slim air currents. Of course he'd prefer to guide the light craft himself — he had the practiced hand of a lover — but regulations forbade manual control when civilian passengers were aboard.

Ironic, since she'd be safer with *him* in control than the automatic pilot. But he hadn't written the rules.

He wasn't even needed, but regulations required the presence of a pilot, in case something went wrong. On automatic, the skimmer maneuvered almost as well as he could do it. Flying in these diffuse, practically non-existent streams of air was tricky. They skirted the downdrafts sometimes encountered on the eastern side of the volcano and headed for the Valles Marineris.

His passenger nudged him and pointed at the bright star hanging above the eastern horizon. "Earth," she whispered.

"The morning star," he added.

"Do you ever want to go back there, Chico?"

He snorted. "Me? Hel — , that is, not at all, ma'am. I have nothing to go back to."

"I have to go back soon. My parents were re-located when the gulf coast washed away, and they need someone to look after them."

*What this woman needs is a man to look after her.* He grunted. It wasn't easy to keep his mouth shut.

His breath flipped the single black curl that always fell over his left eye. He'd learned long ago that obliging the right people and controlling his tongue would get him into places that would otherwise bar him. He could be just as agreeable as he had to be. But there were limits to how long he could behave.

Following the sight lines of the morning star, the skimmer sailed between the two southernmost volcanoes of the Tharsis threesome. The pock trio, he called them. They reminded him of the pocks that scarred Uncle Jota's ugly face. That son of a bitch had tried everything to prevent his illegitimate nephew from getting into the Academy, but it hadn't been enough. Chico had shown him.

Suddenly, the sun burst over the horizon, spilling a golden halo into the darkness. Earth flickered out, as if *Dios* had flipped the light switch, severing his connection to the homeland. *As it should be.*

Then the red came up. Shades of red in the rock-strewn, crater-pocked plains: red-brown, red-orange, red-pink. Everywhere, red invaded everything. Red soil, redder rocks. A wisp of a cloud high above gashed relief in a sky that looked like something out of a virtual world.

"Chico?"

Boss-lady cocked her head at him, and he realized with a wave of horror that his attention had drifted. Only for a moment, and what did it matter, anyway, being on automatic? But it had drifted nonetheless, suggesting to him the hint of a flaw. He was less of a pilot than he'd thought. He snapped back to attention.

"Is that canal up there the beginning of the rift system?" she asked.

He snorted at her mistake, but hell, she was Ms. Administrator. What was she supposed to know?

The chasm opened up ahead of them, making the Grand Canyon back home look like an arroyo. This channel with its jagged, red walls twisted ahead of them, stretching to the horizon and beyond. The craft swooped down into the Martian slash, and Chico felt a moment of light-headedness as the bottom dropped out from under them.

"What the hell?" Automatic pilot would never program a thrill ride, he thought, clutching the controls, punching them to manual.

"Chico!" Boss-lady screamed, bracing herself against the control panel.

The green lights in his lens suddenly blinked out, and along with them, the daylight reaching feebly into this canyon disappeared. Something doused all light, and he felt the pull of the craft as it dropped in altitude. Without the stat display, he had to use his instinct to determine their position, falling to the bottom with a speed and a heaviness that felt greater than the gravitational pull that should come from this lightweight planet. They spiraled down in a pit of black.

Where was the red, *chingada* planet?

"Chico, what's happening?"

He grunted in reply as he wrestled with the throttle, listened for a whine from the engines, evaluated his dizziness to determine their attitude, blinked to clear the fuzz from his vision. Then, as abruptly as the black shadow had taken them in a chokehold, the red, jagged walls of the canyon suddenly appeared, soaring dangerously up on either side of the craft. Now the throttle responded, and he brought the skimmer out of its spiraling fall and into a stable, horizontal swoop.

They'd had time. The bottomland wasn't *that* close beneath them. Still, he could see the details of its buckles, the slivers of rock formations thrusting upward as if to block their passage through the canyon.

"What happened?" Her voice still shrieked.

"Damned if I know. Er, that is, ma'am, we appeared to pass through a, uh, disturbance in the atmosphere. Yes, that's it. It's common to encounter a shift in the air currents when we enter the canyon."

*Goddamn, that was some shift!*

"411, come in!" The duty man at Port Lowell shouted over the com, at the same time that cool, green lights returned in his lens. "Torres, what the hell are you doing? Why'd you take your skimmer off automatic?"

"Switching back," Chico said in his monotonal pilot's voice, even though his heart was still hammering. "You have any information on that disturbance back there?"

"Disturbance? Negative on that."

Chico guessed that a team was already scrambling to investigate the echoes of whatever had nearly happened back there. Of course they'd deny any danger existed. They wouldn't want to alarm the passenger.

He glanced over at her. "Everything's under control," he said, trying his best to make his brusque words sound gentle.

"*You* did that, didn't you?" she said. "You get a perverse thrill out of trying to scare me?"

"No, I swear — "

"I've heard about you, you know. When are you going to grow up?"

"Listen, it wasn't me. Something took hold of us. Didn't you feel it?"

She cocked her head at him, and when she spoke again, the fire was gone from her voice. "Maybe coming here was a mistake." She looked around, as if searching for an exit.

"Take it easy, we're almost there."

She let out a long sigh and leaned back in her seat as the skimmer dipped and dove and swept along the whimsical curves of the ancient flow that had once carved this planet. For once, he was glad to turn over control of the craft to automatic.

"411." The voice from Port Lowell suddenly filled the tiny cockpit. "We've lost contact with Valles Marineris."

"Roger, copy. Will check it out from here." Chico flipped the channel to the science station, so new it was still under construction at the base of the solar system's greatest canyon. He tried them several times, but there was no response.

He tensed, peered ahead as the craft sliced through the red canyon, then made up his mind and switched to manual control. He didn't want to be taken by surprise again. He slowed their speed, but his mind stayed on alert for another... Not a disturbance. What could he call it? He felt a shudder pass silently through him.

*Jesucristo.*

Watching for more shadows, for anything that might take him unaware, he stared intently at their course through the arroyo. Nothing. Ahead, the canyon bent, and sunlight shafted into its depths. In the distance he could see Mylar glinting, a silvery parasite attached to a shadowy, red corner where walls met the canyon floor. He slowed the skimmer to a cautious drift on its final approach, then circled above the construction site of ISA's newest habitat.

"Doesn't look like they've made much progress," Boss-lady said, her voice breaking.

"That's not lack of progress, ma'am," Chico said, his fingers twitching. The Mylar bubbles should be inflated. Not shredded into a mound of rubble. "Looks like there's been an explosion."

Just then, a dust cloud mushroomed up from the debris, rising bullet fast toward the skimmer. Chico's bones vibrated. The craft rocked, and the bottom dropped out again. "Hang on!" he shouted as they plunged to the floor of the canyon.

———

ZIZA FONSECA STOOD NAKED in the heart of the jungle. Her mother's crazy followers surrounded her, ogling her, oohing and ahhing. They reached for her, tickling her firm flesh, and the platform where they all crowded, dipped and tilted in the swampy waters.

Ziza had sworn that she would never come back home to Amazonas, and yet here she was. All because of the bonus Doctor Inez had promised in exchange for the secret recording.

Quick as a serpent, her mother grabbed Ziza's arm and pried open her fingers hiding the camera card. "What is this?"

"Nothing, Mãe," Ziza said, a stammering child once again. "It's...just my identification. From the city. That is all." Heat rose to her cheeks, whether from the lie or the overwhelming perfume of the moonrose, she couldn't tell.

Ziza felt her mother's grip tighten on her arm. She stood on tiptoes to put her face in Ziza's face. "You dishonor me. You, who ran away to the foreigners."

With a strength greater than her shriveled frame would indicate, Mãe wrenched the card from Ziza's fingers and flung it away from the platform. A distant plink told Ziza what her mother thought of her job with the foreigners. Good thing there was still a microphone planted in her navel.

"We will make everything right now," Mãe said with a grin that showed off her missing front teeth. With one hand she reached for the flask that was passing from woman to woman, and with the other, grabbed Ziza's long braid.

"No...what are you doing?" Ziza twisted, trying to shake off her mother's work, but she felt as powerless as the moonrose vine, hacked from the tree with a machete by one of the women.

"You thought you could run away from your dance of puberty, did you?" Mãe said, yanking her head back. She tipped the flask to Ziza's lips. Some of its contents dribbled down her chin. The drops that made it into her throat burned like hell.

Turpentine? She couldn't quite place it. She remembered days long past, days from her childhood in the shanty town downriver, watching the shaman at work in the market. A mish-mash of canvas canopy flapped over stacks of rotting, wooden crates that divided the place into a maze of stalls. That's where the shaman worked, dipping his fingers into partially-full barrels of the ingredients he needed to prepare the concoction for Mãe's Mundomba women. Pulverized teeth from unknown animals. Bark and roots and slimy leaves. He squirted drops and sprinkled powders into the brew, then chanted meaningless sounds over the bubbling froth. Finally, he stuffed the mixture into a gouged fish, bound it tightly in an anaconda's skin, and hung it up to ferment for three full moon cycles.

That brew was what Mãe forced down Ziza's throat. Ziza coughed it all back up. Her spray sent Mãe's women ducking.

The wooden platform began to rock. Or was it her imagination? She burned with the fire of the brew that had wormed its way inside. Women surrounding her writhed. Bare arms uplifted, glistening with sweat. Fingers twitched. With eyes closed, the women invoked the heavens. Their sing-song chant stirred the night prowlers to a background clamor.

A moan sliced through the crowd, as one of the women placed the high priestess's garland of fish skulls round Mãe's neck. Frenzy slipped away from the women as they fell back, forming a wide semi-circle around Mãe, their healer leader.

Mãe dropped her shriveled arms and stilled. Likewise, did her throng of followers. Insects missed a beat of their background samba, as if sensing a change in the air. The wood stopped shaking beneath Ziza's feet, but water continued to stir against the boards. She felt dizzy, floating, mesmerized like the others. Women's faces watched in the silvery light, waiting for the cue. Mãe's wrinkled flesh began rippling under shuddery waves. Then her eyes rolled back into her head, leaving only the whites exposed in a face more black than night.

With head laid back and whites of her eyes shining in the moonlight, Mãe the priestess reached blindly for the hacked vine of the moonrose, then wrapped the vine around her drooping bosom and uttered sing-song sounds in a raspy voice. The priestess sang, and the wailing, off-beat sound sent tingles rippling through Ziza. The cadence, the tone, the rhythm pulled at the women like a ceaseless undertow. Deep, sucking sounds rolled through them as time stopped around them. And with each gush came sounds that might've been words. Words Ziza had never heard, could not recognize, and she trembled with fever as the night wore on.

Vines tangled the shriveled body of the ageless woman, her mother, the priestess. The song she sang finally choked itself off, then Mãe unrolled her eyes, a signal for the end of the ritual. Silence fell heavy over the Mundomba women on the platform. Ziza, shrinking into a fetal ball at their feet, startled to see fingers of rosy light slipping through the holes in the jungle ceiling. The remains of the moonroses wilted into limp nubs, as finished as the night. And the women. Their energy spent, they lifted Ziza to her feet and patted her on the back.

With a sinking feeling of dread, Ziza knew. She was Mundomba now.

Something glimmered in the priestess's eyes and drool trickled from the corners of her mouth. Her knobby hands twitched, and she stumbled to her knees. Unblinking, she stared up at Ziza. Purple colored her face, and her toothless mouth gaped open.

"Mãe?" This ritual was over, Ziza thought, reaching for the old woman to give her a shake.

Her mother gasped, and someone else's voice spoke-sang through Mãe's mouth. "We are... Tititri. We... come..." She clawed at her bare throat and choked one last time, then crashed to a lifeless heap on the platform.

"Mãe!" Ziza screamed.

# Chapter Two

WALKER FROWNED AT THE STATUS SCREENS blinking across his desk. His lab sat on the outer rim of SpaceHab, and he could almost feel the steady cycle of the wheel beneath him, sweeping him ever onward. Never forward.

"It sounds like someone's voice," he said, adjusting the volume. "Probably a reflection of one of our early transmission tests."

Faint blips interjected into the sounds of static issuing from the speakers while a visual display scrolled before him. Graphs showed the record of the external equipment's capture of the tachyonic burst. A collector out there had caught the subatomic particles that moved faster than the speed of light, and now the converter was presenting that capture into auditory and visual data that could be analyzed.

"That's what I thought, too, at first," said Jackson, his assistant. "It should be a reflection."

Walker's fingers paused on the volume. "What changed your mind?"

"Look at where it's coming from. Given the orbital status of all our transmitters, none of them could've intersected the trajectory of this particular stream of tachyons."

"There's an explanation," Walker said. "There's always an explanation. We just haven't found it yet. How about the other labs? Anyone else report capturing a sample of this burst?"

"Not yet."

Walker fell silent, his way of dealing with disappointment. He studied the array of equipment. He'd spent his career building it, modifying it, refining it. He'd captured tachyonic bursts before that hadn't come from any of their outposts. He'd fed them into the converter and analyzed them. None of them had attached any sounds suggesting voices. If this wasn't a reflection, then what was it?

He scowled at the display and straightened his shoulders as he came to a decision. "Okay, here's what I want you to do. Run a full diagnostic on all the equipment, starting with the collector — "

"We'll have to send someone outside on an EVA for that."

"Right. And when you're done, then start on the converter. Check out every piece of equipment, including the tachcom. Something's not reading right, and we're going to find it." More than anything, Walker hated mistakes.

"That's going to take some time. We might lose what we've collected so far, if we have to open up the equipment outside."

"That's the risk we'll have to take."

One of the techs waited patiently nearby and cleared his throat. "Sorry to interrupt."

"What?" As soon as he spit out the word, Walker felt a flush rise to his face. He swiped his hand across his close-cropped hair, then softened his voice. Always making amends. "Yes, Anders?"

"Sir, we've got a coded transmission from headquarters. The chief himself. Urgent, he says."

With H.F. Washington, director of the International Space Agency, it was always urgent. "Okay. I'll take it here." He swiveled around to the viewscreen where he flipped a secure channel open to fuzzy reception.

"Landon, my boy," said the man on the screen. Gray hair bushed around his shoulders. Deep lines etched across his tired face, dragging his jaw line, once firm and square, into a withered shape, a mass of old man's wrinkles.

"H.F., what's up?" A surge of alarm coursed through Walker. He couldn't remember his boss ever looking so tired. So defeated.

H.F.'s image flickered out, replaced by scratchy interference. Scrambling to adjust the controls, Walker wondered where the director's high energy had gone. H.F. Washington was the man most responsible for making ISA the largest and most profitable space consortium that it was today, the man who'd realized his dreams by building SpaceHab, Lunar Observatory, and Port Lowell.

H.F.'s weary face returned. "...having a few people in for cocktails," he was saying amidst static. "...insist that you come."

Walker felt himself tighten at the mention of the director's favorite code. That meant H.F. was calling an emergency meeting at headquarters, the Goiás facility, and it was top secret.

"You're asking me to leave my lab *now*?" Walker said. He'd already sent H.F. the preliminary report, hand-delivered by courier, and Walker couldn't explain any better to H.F. in person than what was in the report. "Um, this isn't the best time, sir."

"Nonsense. The shuttle will be there for you in a couple of hours."

Walker kneaded his neck. "I'm in the middle of...er, a routine test." He had to be careful. The "Savers," that renegade band of terrorists, monitored their transmissions and even decoded some of their most secure messages. All under the warped belief that they were saving the Earth from ecological disaster by destroying technology.

"That's precisely the point," H.F. said, leaning a little closer to his transmitter. "A few of my guests are anxious to meet you." He coughed. "They might be able to contribute a few insights regarding your situation."

Walker glanced from right to left, looking for inspiration that would explain to H.F. why he couldn't oblige him. But he came up with nothing convincing. He wasn't exactly busy. Jackson was competent enough to carry on monitoring the diagnostics of the equipment here during Walker's absence.

Walker rubbed his forehead, suddenly feeling as tired as H.F. looked on the screen. He wondered what his boss had in mind that was more important than this lab's work. The director never dreamed of small projects.

"You've been working too hard," H.F. continued. "You need a little break, and we need you here."

Jackson nudged him and whispered, "He's right, you know."

H.F. gave a wan smile, but the effort only made his eyelids droop. "Is there a problem, my boy?"

Walker glared at his assistant, then turned back to the screen with a sigh. He didn't need any help from anyone to know what he had to do. H.F. had found the grant money that made Walker's entire career of research into tachyonic communications possible. The old man always believed in him, even when no one else did.

Now Walker had to believe in H.F. Trust him. Leaning back in his chair, he shook his head. "No problem, sir."

The director laughed, a baritone sound coming from deep within his diaphragm. "That's it? Landon, my boy, for a communications expert, you don't say much, do you?"

Walker smiled faintly at the familiar ribbing. "I'll be ready for the shuttle."

————

SWEAT TRICKLED DOWN Walker's forehead, stinging his eyes and giving him a welcome sense of direction. It was the only welcome aspect of this trip in the private shuttle that the International Space Agency had sent for him. Pressure bound him to his couch as they pushed into the tenuous layer of Earth's atmosphere. Pockets inflated and squeezed his thighs with an unrelenting grip. Pink enshrouded all six of this shuttle's tiny windows.

*Twelve minutes*, Walker thought. That's how long it would take the craft to burn its way through the atmosphere. Air molecules smashed against the little vehicle with the roar of demons, screaming to get inside, where the com panel remained silent under this electromagnetic shroud.

After all the times he'd shuttled down, he never could get used to this fiery return. Missions were reaching farther and farther away from home in more and more comfortable spaceships, but these final twelve minutes, these critical minutes of life or death, never grew easier.

Walker balled his fists and counted off the time in his head. Three, four... Filling his mind with an exercise in distraction was the only way to get through it. He reminded himself that there hadn't been a mistake in half a century, not since private enterprise had replaced the crippled NASA. Forty-five, forty-six... The two-man crew, the only other occupants of the shuttle, continued their monotonal checklist as if being smothered by a burning atmosphere and cut off from communication were everyday occurrences. Walker tried to swallow but couldn't.

Suddenly, static sounded over the com, then a voice. *"Aquarius,* welcome home."

Walker let out his breath, not realizing he'd been holding it. He stared out the window at the Pacific glinting through the remnants of pink haze. The ocean looked calm, but it never was, really. Just like any abyss, waiting to swallow him.

The shuttle's speed made the Pacific and its world seem smaller than he knew it to be. Already ahead, the South American cordillera rose like green fingers from the sea. The shuttle skimmed toward it, swooping through curves that brought the horizon into constantly shifting, vertical positions. Walker's stomach churned. Finally, that curving line leveled, where Earth met sky, not space, and it looked again the way a horizon should. But Walker's queasiness wouldn't settle. Now they were dropping rapidly over the peaks, where mountain air currents caught them and flung them about, reminding them that Nature was still the force in control. He braced himself as they sank alarmingly low to the final rises in only a matter of seconds. Green gave way to barren, reddish plains.

Before it seemed possible, a jolt rippled through his tensed muscles. "Touchdown," the pilot commented, void of emotion.

Red dust mushroomed past, and Walker suffered a moment of disorientation. For an instant it seemed as if the burning ride through the atmosphere had led him back in time to Mars, where, as the golden boy in H.F.'s lab, he'd built the prototype of his tachcom. It was the beginning of his work investigating instantaneous communication. Another lifetime ago.

"Here you are, Dr. Walker," one of the pilots said. "ISA headquarters, Goiás, Brazil."

Walker's teeth rattled against each other, jarring from him any remnants of those happy memories from Port Lowell. He didn't need memories any more. They only interfered with his real work. He concentrated instead on the vibrations tickling his body. Pressure shoved his head back, and weight hung over him like a lead blanket.

"Please remain seated until the craft comes to a complete stop." The pilots broke out into guffaws, the first hint of any levity since they'd strapped him in a couple of hours ago.

Walker scowled at them. He didn't need levity, either. These were serious times. His entire future hung on that tachyonic emission streaming into his collector at SpaceHab. He should be back there analyzing it, not here, answering H.F.'s questions. Odd, though. The director had never micromanaged before.

When the shuttle finally rolled to a stop and the pilots busied themselves powering down systems, he worked at his bindings. His fingers moved awkwardly, off target. He looked up long enough to glance out at the surrounding Brazilian no-man's land. A dust cloud in the distance indicated something moving toward the shuttle. Beyond that, green etched the horizon. Only minutes ago they were grazing the peaks of the Andes and now he couldn't even see them.

Before he shook off the last of the inflated pockets and bindings, however, one pilot was out of his seat and unfastening the hatch. The other pilot hoisted Walker up to his feet. Walker never felt as heavy anywhere as he felt here in Brazil.

With the hatch opened, mugginess seeped inside. It seemed a paradox that moisture could exist here, but he reminded himself that the plateau of Goiás wasn't truly a desert. If you looked closely enough, you would still find stubby remains of a scraggly vegetation.

*Man-made wasteland.*

Having lived most of his life off-planet, he never thought much about mankind's mis-use of the Earth. Not until moments like these. Seeing land each time he returned to Earth was like a slap of heat-scoured air. Ignoring the knot in his stomach, he reminded himself that disasters usually caused technology to leap ahead to new levels. And Landon Walker would be at the leading edge of this technological revolution, in spite of his ex-wife's betrayal. Yes, *this* was his opportunity. Amazing, the progress man could make once a crisis had gone too far.

Standing in the open hatch, held up like a puppet by the pilots, he thought he was going to melt inside his regulation coveralls. Heat blasted his face as if he stood in front of the open door of a furnace. The heat radiated from the central plateau, a flat, red sea, barren except for the thin green line and a cluster of white buildings on the horizon. He watched the dust cloud advance toward them. The pilots clasped hands, in a congratulatory salute, and Walker took advantage of their self-preoccupation to escape. Always ruled by their egos. Did they think he couldn't walk? He stumbled down the steps to show them he was just as fit as they, even though he was old enough to be their...maybe their older brother. Sure, he was aging, having passed the half-century mark. Not old, and certainly not beyond usefulness.

Footsteps clattered down the ramp behind Walker, and the three space travelers stepped onto the parched soil of Earth. An automated cart, the first of several arriving vehicles, slowed its mag lev suspension ride and floated down to the blistering surface of Earth. The dust cloud that the cart's passage had stirred drifted past them long after four people sprang down from the vehicle's open sides. Two of them, mechanics, headed for the underbelly of the shuttle. The third was a guard who scanned their surroundings with a smart weapon. A fourth passenger, a lean woman, attractive in a slick, no-nonsense way despite the baggy, ISA coveralls she wore, marched over to Walker and the pilots. She singled out Walker and grinned at him with a smile that showed off radiant teeth against a deeply tanned face.

"Dr. Walker?" she said, extending her hand. Her fingers were so slim in his grip that he thought instantly of the baby's clasp. He tried to release himself from the handshake, but she wouldn't let go until she was ready.

Dropping his hand finally, she nodded at the pilot in charge. "Captain."

"Doctor," the pilot responded. Their voices lowered into the cold range.

"Nice flight, gentlemen?" She waited for them to confirm, then turned back to Walker, who noticed a slight grimace through her mask of efficiency. "I'm Inez Pereira." She spoke English with a pleasant accent suggesting origins in this part of the world. "It is truly an honor to meet you, Dr. Walker. I've admired your research for a long time."

Pereira paused, while a rush of unbidden pleasure from her endorsement surged within him. He rubbed his neck, where he felt the flush spreading. "Well, ma'am, you're very kind, considering that not everyone shares your opinion."

She waved away his protest. "Your research will make space travel more accessible. Colonization of space becomes a real option with instantaneous communication."

"That's what we hope," he said. "But it's not the primary reason that potential colonists will sign up for H.F.'s new habitats."

"You're too modest, Dr. Walker. She smiled as if she knew a secret, something he couldn't be expected to know.

"Look, what's this meeting all about?" he asked, trying to suppress his irritation.

"Yes, you're right," Pereira said. "Let's get on with it. This way, please."

She motioned him toward the vehicle in which she'd arrived, but suddenly, her arm dropped to her side and her slender body stiffened. Alert, she stared off to the west. Walker followed her gaze and thought he saw something sparkle briefly against the wasted background. Before he could determine what the speck was, however, the guard shouted.

"Take cover!"

Pereira pounced on Walker and shoved him toward the cart. He stumbled and started to fall, but before his knees could touch the red soil, the woman grabbed him by the elbow with a strength that surprised him for her slight build.

The spot on the ground where he'd stood a moment before suddenly flew apart in a spray of red clumps. A bullet, not a missile, judging from the narrow diameter of the exploding ring. A deadly bullet, all the same.

# Chapter Three

*S*HE WAS SWIMMING THROUGH A SEA *of ice, whispering watery ice, seeking...*

"Greer."

*...the passage to... She couldn't remember.*

"Greer, wake up."

*No, it was too soon. She had to find...whatever it was that she'd lost... Was she lost?*

"She's thawed. Why isn't she waking up?"

*Chills coursed through her. Ice pulsed through her veins.*

"Give her five cc's of A-Narcant."

*So cold in here. She wanted to massage warmth into her arms, but she couldn't make her fingers work. She tried to flex them, but she couldn't even feel them. Did she have fingers?*

"Not so close. Give her space."

*An explosion rocked through her. The Dome, shattering into pieces... Daddy! Landie!*

"That's good. We're getting a response."

*A violent shiver possessed her. Spasms shot through her body, spasms she couldn't control. Unwanted, like flashes of memories. Fingers of ice probed her. Pain needled through her veins. Cold... So cold...*

"Come on, Greer honey, open your eyes."

At first, all she could see was a face peering down at her, filling the space above her. Soft light illuminated the face, light too soft to enable her to recognize the stranger's face.

"Welcome back," the face said. It belonged to a bald woman. It was a sharp face with angular features and a pinched nose. The face looked vaguely familiar, but Greer wasn't sure. Something felt wrong.

Greer opened her mouth to ask. Just what the hell was happening? Maybe it was her? But only a gasp escaped. Her throat felt raw and cracked.

"There is someone who says he must see you." The bald woman spoke with a nasal twang and an accent that swallowed her words. "How do you feel?"

How did she feel? She felt...nothing. That is, nothing besides the cold. She was a drifting awareness, a thought process out of body.

Another face, a man's, stepped closer, into her field of vision. "Why doesn't she say anything?"

"Not to worry," the bald one said. "Everything is normal for the post-cryonic state. She needs a little more time coming out."

Greer drifted again, and then something buzzed. Pesky damned insects. Got to use bug bombs... They're environmentally sound and, after all, the world was full of mutated species of bugs, so bombs were okay to use. She shuddered. Had she been stung? So cold in here...

Voices floated out of the buzzing. "...Slipping again...got to bring her back *now*..."

She felt the slap of a warm cloth on her forehead. She opened her eyes and realized that what she was hearing was not insects but rather their echo in her head. And urgent voices. Whispering.

"Damnation," the bald woman said, stomping around the room where Greer slowly gained awareness.

She lay in a tank of some sort. Her skin itched. She tried to lift her hand to rub her temples, to rub away the metal lugs dotting her scalp, but her arm was too heavy.

"Impatient, are we?" The bald woman brushed her fingers away from the tangle of wires. "You're not going anywhere yet, no matter what he says. You mustn't disconnect yourself."

Greer's eyelids sagged with the crush of returning memory. "Doctor..." she whispered. Husky, but her voice worked. "Dr. Montague."

Renee Montague was director of the cryonics treatment center. *That's* what was wrong. Why wasn't a techie bringing Greer out of cryo sleep instead of the person in charge of the whole place?

"Yes, Greer?" Dr. Montague leaned closer.

"Did it...work okay?"

"Like a charm."

"Then...I'm still twenty-nine?"

"And holding. But we did have to wake you up sooner than the treatment specified in your contract. You have a visitor, and he will explain. He's here from the world court with an order of some kind."

Greer knew it. Something had gone wrong. A chill swept through her, but this time she couldn't blame post-cryonics for her shivers.

# Chapter Four

WALKER SHOWERED BRIEFLY in his ISA guest quarters, but it didn't wash away his unease. The memory of the attack rang through him as water ran off him.

"Security alert to strip three." That's what Pereira had said, once she'd shoved him inside the automated cart, calling for reinforcements.

The woman had just saved his life! And that's all she thought it was? A security alert?

Walker still shuddered at any mention of a breach of security. The Savers, his ex-wife's whack-o band of conspirators, had tried — and failed, thank god — to blow up SpaceHab. And long before that, a security breach in the Vancouver Dome had killed his father. Hadn't those types done enough damage?

But Pereira brushed off this latest attack as nothing. "Angry locals," she'd explained. "A few of them break through our perimeters from time to time. Security will take care of them."

He didn't believe a word of it. How could anyone manage to slip past ISA's fence of criss-crossed laser beams and fire that bullet at him, if that's what it was? No. Penetrating such a barrier would require smart weapons. Today's attacker, however, didn't have a smart weapon. If he'd had one, then Walker would be a dead man right now.

Someone from the inside must've let in the sniper with the traditional rifle. Was that what Pereira was lying about? Because she knew? Because she was covering up what she knew?

By the time Walker finished showering and dressing, he'd managed to control his shaking. He exited the guest quarters and found that no one awaited him. Fine. Being on his own suited him. Instead of an escort, an artificial voice and arrowing wall lights led him through the maze of corridors and past offices, research labs, models of habitats, and assembly rooms. All of this served as support for the newest spaceships under construction that would help fulfill H.F.'s quest to open new frontiers.

"Your destination, sir," the voice said, ushering him into a conference room.

A large, oval table of gleaming, white plastic filled the room. Opposite the door was a bay of windows where H.F. stood, contemplating the barren landscape outside. With his hands behind his broad back, he fingered a chain of amber beads.

"H.F!" Walker exclaimed with a momentary lapse, showing excitement. He rushed into the room.

The man at the window turned and beamed at him. "Good to see you, my boy." He strode over to him with arms extended, like a father greeting a long-lost son, and clasped Walker by the shoulders. "I understand you had a bit of excitement just now. Are you sure you're all right?"

Walker nodded. "I'll live. But someone trying to kill me is not my definition of excitement."

H.F. laughed his deep, rumbling laugh. "On the contrary. Don't flatter yourself. They were after *Aquarius*, not you."

"The Savers are better shots than that."

"Not Savers," H.F. said, shaking his head. "It was a local. One of the squatters outside our boundaries."

"Ah, you found him, then?"

"No, he got away, but I'm telling you, it had to be a squatter."

"Why would one of your locals care enough to take out *Aquarius*?"

H.F. shrugged and moved swiftly to a small bar. "Maybe he didn't like our noise, who knows? What's important is that there's no real harm done. Good thing you had Dr. Pereira with you."

Walker's unease rumbled through him again. H.F. was usually oblivious to any collateral damage going on around him when one of his pet projects consumed him. Walker felt certain that he'd been the target today, not the *Aquarius*. Killing him, the Savers must think, would serve as retaliation for his ex-wife's imprisonment. As if Walker were to blame, just because he hadn't fought for her, hadn't tried to get her off.

"Amazing woman, that one," H.F. continued, examining his assortment of bottles. "My discovery."

His ex-wife? Walker stiffened, then realized that his attention had wandered again and H.F. was talking about that woman who'd met him today. His pulse throbbed uncomfortably. Whatever secret Pereira had been lying to protect, it better not have to do with betraying H.F. Walker would see to that.

"I found her," H.F. said, "working in some linguist's office down in Rio. She was with a project studying the languages of Amazonian tribes."

"What's she doing here?" Walker could think of no practical reason why an Amazonian linguist should be employed by the world's leading space entrepreneur. But H.F. would have a reason to own her. The old man always had a reason.

"She'll be joining us later for our meeting, but for now she's tied up with some business of her own. We'll start, anyway, as soon as the rest of them arrive." H.F. glanced at his wristwatch, as anachronistic as the man himself, a man who favored the styles of the previous century in spite of his visions for the future.

"What others?" Walker said. "Who are they? What's this all about?"

"Patience, my boy." H.F. selected a bottle from his bar and poured two shots. "You and I have other items to catch up on first."

"Such as, letting me know why you've called this emergency meeting? Did that squatter's complaint back there at strip three have anything to do with this meeting?"

H.F. waved off his questions and handed him a glass. "Scotch?"

Annoyed, Walker shook his head.

"It's not what you think," H.F. said. "This is a celebration. Besides, you — especially you — will need a little help relaxing. Perhaps I can offer you something else to drink? Champagne?"

Walker let out a long breath. "Iced tea. With a twist of lemon."

H.F. slapped him on the back. "Still drinking the same hard stuff, are you?"

Walker scowled and turned away. He had no wish to numb his mind. Waiting while glass and ice chinked behind him, he studied the open landscape outside the windows. ISA owned all of it, all the scorched land he could see, and more. The laser fence surrounded the entire Goiás facility, an area five times the size of the legendary Cape Canaveral, a place that had been beneath water for a couple of decades.

Had one of the guards de-activated the fence today? It would only take a blink of time for someone unauthorized and disgruntled to get through.

He felt a nudge at his elbow and turned. H.F. extended a frosty tumbler and sighed. "Have you heard the news yet? The news out of Port Lowell?"

"No. Have they confirmed my readings?" Walker hoped so. The failure of other labs to duplicate a functional tachcom made his work seem invalid. Surely, someone else could pick up this highly collectible stream of tachyons.

H.F. shook his head. "It's bad, I'm afraid."

"What is it?" Walker thought for a minute that the old man was going to be sick. "Have they lost their funding?"

"It's far worse than that. Accident. The new lab site we were constructing in the Valles Marineris is a total loss. Investigators are sifting through the rubble now."

Walker stiffened. "What kind of accident?"

"An explosion, apparently, but it's too early to tell. Although, there was a report of an unusual emission that passed through the area."

"So it was a deliberate target?" Probably another "security alert," Walker thought with an involuntary shudder, only this one hadn't missed as today's had. "Sabotage?"

31

"No one escaped."

"That doesn't necessarily mean it wasn't an inside job," Walker said. "Savers haven't penetrated Port Lowell, too, have they?"

"It's not Savers. Forget the Savers. Savers are all but defeated these days. We conveniently blame them anytime there's an accident, but really, their organization is too weak to be effective anymore. You spend too much time off Earth."

Walker bristled. "The media keeps me informed." Besides, he knew for a fact that his ex-wife had been recruited by Savers. She'd been ripe for their brainwashing thanks to that back-to-nature cult she'd joined long-distance from SpaceHab. How ironic was that?

"The media tells you what they want you to know," H.F. said, wagging his eyebrows. He thumbed through his worry beads, clicking them loudly as if to underscore his opinion.

"You're not suggesting the media is behind this?" Walker said.

H.F. grinned. "If that were true, then it would already be over."

"*What* would be over?" Walker tugged at his collar, although it wasn't hot in this climate-controlled building. "You pulled me away from my work to play games with me?"

"Quite simply, I need your help. We have an urgent situation on our hands, and your emission is only the beginning."

One of Walker's eyebrows shot up.

"I'm assembling the worlds' top minds on these matters." H.F. continued. "We are on the cutting edge of breakthroughs in our limited understanding. We are about to join our galactic cousins in understanding that which has eluded us throughout the history of mankind."

Walker shook his head. *Galactic cousins!* "You think aliens sent that emission that killed those people on Mars?"

"Is that so hard to believe? You yourself saw the ruins on Titan. I sent you there. Remember?"

Sure. He remembered. "They're dead. Gone. Extinct. We can't have any first contact if they're dead."

H.F. glared at him.

Walker swiped one hand across his face in frustration and went on. "Look. Whoever built those objects on Titan, wherever they came from, that has nothing to do with this. Just because they existed at one time doesn't mean that aliens sent the emission I captured three days ago. If that's what you think, it's simply not true. I don't know what hit Mars, but the emission my lab captured couldn't do that. It's only an echo. Of my own work. It's all in my report. You didn't have to pull me out of my lab for *this*."

H.F. took a long swallow of his drink. "Maybe it's not an echo."

"Oh, come on, what else can it be?"

"I remind you that this signal is coming from Alpha Centauri."

"It's an emission, not a signal."

"And it's coming from the future," H.F. said.

"I beg your pardon?"

"If tachyons are faster than light particles," the director said, "then your message is coming from the future, am I right?"

Walker thrust one fist into his pocket. "Maybe. Or the past. Simplistically speaking, of course. But you should ask Van Pelt. Theory is his area, not mine."

"Your tachcom could be a time machine, couldn't it?" H.F. asked, his voice dropping.

"That's one way to think about it."

"Then, you've breached time itself, whether you call it an emission or a signal." He poured himself another shot, then recapped the bottle. "You deserve congratulations."

"Don't I wish?" Walker said with a sigh. "See here, this emission may be coming from *us* in the future, but it's not coming from aliens. You're wrong, if that's what you're thinking."

"You know that for a fact?"

"I'll admit that the emission doesn't look exactly like one of ours, but that doesn't necessarily mean it's E.T.'s."

"You know what your trouble is, my boy? You're so fixated on the nuts and bolts of your machine that you can't see beyond its mechanical parts.

You can't see the potential. Why do you think I'm interested in tachyonic research, anyway?"

Walker frowned. "Some people are willing to pay big money for instantaneous communication."

"You're right about the big money part," H.F. said, "and it's going to get even bigger. A talking device is only the beginning. Our E.T. has probably gone far beyond our primitive steps."

Walker snorted. "Forget E.T. E.T. is long dead and gone. We haven't found any extraterrestrial organisms currently alive that are more complex than bacteria."

"*Yet*. But we'll find them."

"We're lucky that we found those ruins. We know now that intelligent life isn't unique in the universe. However, each rise and fall of a civilization is a mere blink in the time scale of the universe. The likelihood of co-existing civilizations within reach of each other is next to nil."

"They're still out there, Landon. For the sake of my argument, let's say their civilization is older than ours. Let's assume it developed tachyonic communication long ago. What's the next step? Travel, by way of tachyonic blueprint of the body — "

"You're taking this too far." How much Scotch had the director had before this one?

H.F. sighed. "We'll continue this discussion later with the others, once they arrive. Perhaps they'll change your mind, since I can't." H.F.'s deep brown eyes bored into Walker's soul. He lowered his voice to a somber tone. "What I really want to know is how you're holding up. And about Summer, of course. How's Summer?"

"Gone," Walker replied curtly, sipping his drink. Better to think that his wife had never existed than to acknowledge the pain she'd left him with.

"I'm sorry, my boy. The life sentence in Patagonia is a little harsh, though, don't you think?"

Walker shrugged.

"And the child?" H.F. persisted.

"With my sister. Greer. In the Holland Annex."

"Good." H.F.'s shaggy brows knitted together, then he repeated the word, as if trying to persuade himself. "Greer will be good for her."

"It can't be helped."

H.F. nodded heartily, his gray mane tossing wildly against slumping shoulders.

Walker took a long swallow of tea in an attempt to quell the burning sensation in his gut. "There was nothing else I could do," he said. The court system had given him sole custody after Summer's deportation, but he couldn't raise a child — not unless he gave up his work.

He'd been desperate at the time. He saw that now. His desperation to carry on with his work had left him blind to any other alternatives regarding care for the child, and so he'd put her in cryo-sleep. That had been his excuse, but it had been a stupid mistake for a baby. Now the world courts were punishing him for his mistake by sending the baby to Greer. That, he feared, was a fate even worse than cryo-sleep.

# Chapter Five

ZIZA FONSECA HADN'T BEEN ABLE to get away fast enough from Mãe's jungle. Now that she was back in Goiás, she felt safe, even though the scientists here acted strangely. They'd summoned her to this meeting today. She didn't know why.

She sensed frenzy in the air, smelling it like a festering sore. Something was brewing at the International Space Agency. Visitors arrived every hour, speaking in whispers. Everyone who lived at ISA rushed off to their summons behind closed doors. The meeting Ziza attended was only one of who knew how many such goings on here today.

It was not for her to know. She was little more than a trainee with Doctor Inez's group, and yet her boss had insisted Ziza come and hear the new assistant director discuss the big new project. Why? It made no sense, unless her boss thought that Ziza could translate something obscure for her, something that would keep her in the discussion. Perhaps the new boss-of-her-boss was Mundomba?

But no. His name was Sam Talcott, a former astronaut, but he didn't look like one, Ziza thought. His confident swagger reminded her of the recruiters who'd ventured into the jungle looking for volunteers for the re-education camps — that's how Ziza had gotten out the first time. Talcott was a fortyish man with thick waves of black hair that sharply contrasted the white-white of his throwback suit. He wore a polished chunk of rose quartz on his collar like a talisman. Ziza felt its power reach to her across the room. She didn't think scientists or astronauts were supposed to respect such powers.

He was delighted to be on board here at Goiás after too long in the field, he told them in his introductory remarks. As H.F. Washington's right-hand man, he was looking forward to working with Doctor Inez's division. Their major new project was of vital importance to the future of humanity.

Ziza didn't know what to believe, but she felt humbled in the presence of such importance. And she felt uneasy that his focus kept drifting toward *her* during his introduction. Uneasier still when she caught the linguists around the table casting surreptitious glances at her, too. As if they expected something of her.

She'd turned over the recording from the microphone in her navel. Whatever happened that night of her mother's death was all recorded. What more did they need from her?

Ziza glanced over at Doctor Inez for reassurance, but she tapped furiously at her datapad, as if searching for some answer she couldn't find.

The linguists didn't always tell her the full story of what they needed from her, but then she was no one in their lab. She'd been training in the Tupi-Guaraní sector of AmerIndian Conservation Inc. down in Rio when her boss, Dr. Inez Pereira, hand-picked her to come up here to Goiás with her, to work for the International Space Agency. Goiás was a lot closer to Mãe's jungle than Rio. Practically neighbors. That proximity made Ziza nervous, but she'd do anything for Doctor Inez.

That's why she'd gone back to the jungle, to the place of her origins, to make the recording. For Doctor Inez. And for the bonus, of course.

Ziza couldn't even grieve for her own mother. Instead, she only felt guilt that she couldn't grieve. Even from death, Ziza's mother possessed her. The first time Ziza had run away from home, she swore that she'd never go back.

But she'd gone back for Doctor Inez, and now look at her. Now she was Mundomba. Mundomba lodged inside Ziza like a parasite.

What exactly happened that night of her mother's death, Ziza didn't know. She'd lost hours of her life. During those lost hours, the power of

Mundomba had reached out and snatched her soul, enfolding her into the cult. She may not like it, but she couldn't deny the power.

With his introduction done, Sam Talcott moved swiftly to the front of the room. There he operated the controls while describing the fact-finding trip from around the world that he'd just completed, his first official assignment for the International Space Agency. Through ISA's network of contacts he'd gathered holograms of sixteen men and women, and he displayed them now, one by one. Ziza's attention riveted to their images on the wallscreen. Even in hologram, their eyes gleamed with fervor and their mouths dribbled with poison.

Like Mãe, Ziza thought.

"What you're seeing," Talcott said in a low voice, "are sixteen madmen from around the world." A soft voice, yet it commanded more attention than Ziza wanted to give him. "Known by a variety of terms: prophets, fortunetellers, soothsayers, witches, shamans, hell, even consultants." He paused again, smirking and waiting for a ripple of laughter from his joke.

Ziza didn't feel like laughing.

"And all sixteen of them are dead now," Talcott continued. "Why is that significant you ask? Subjects of this type are usually homeless, drifting from one potential resource to the next, living on the good graces of their fanatic followers. They experience constant adversity, and the more meaningful question is why do they live as long as they do." He paced, deep in thought, as if speaking to himself. He rattled coins in his pockets.

"It's significant," he said, "because of the similarities. In each case these sixteen experienced a grand moll type seizure and then raved in an unknown tongue immediately before collapsing, dead. While we don't understand what they uttered, and in each case it was an unknown language, it seems to contain the same message."

At this mention, the team leaders round the table exchanged glances. Eyebrows shot up.

Mario Renato, section leader for the Uminoya family of dialects, frowned over the rim of his half-glasses. "Obviously, the language wasn't completely unknown if you recognized enough of it to understand that what each of them was speaking was the same."

Doctor Inez leaned over and whispered something to Renato, who frowned and shook his head.

Talcott went on, stroking his chin while he stared at Ziza. "We understand there is a seventeenth case, a local connection. Alas, we have no visuals." He clicked to the next window. "Why do we care about the deaths of madmen? Because of the message they deliver. This exhibit that you're looking at now illustrates the pattern of prime numbers we were able to extract from their, er, presentations, if you will. It's interesting to note that in all seventeen cases the pattern was the same. We have experts in another lab working on it now. But what is pertinent for this group is the language. In all seventeen cases, death followed the acquisition of said language."

"Are you suggesting," asked Lura Santos, one of Doctor Inez's assistants, "that we have an unknown language that causes death?"

An eruption of voices spread through the room. Talcott rocked on his heels and waited.

"People," Doctor Inez said, tapping her stylus against her water glass. "Let Dr. Talcott finish, and then he'll take your questions."

But Lura continued before order could resettle. "This is all very interesting, but first we have to determine if what you have here is actually a valid language and not the result of hallucinatory rantings. It's not language until it's two-way."

What Ziza wanted to know, but didn't have the courage to voice since she didn't really belong here with these scientists, was why the *space* agency was involved in unknown languages.

Talcott gazed at Ziza, as if reading her thoughts, while answering Lura. "Precisely. In a nutshell, you have nailed the focus of your project: who is their audience? Who speaks their language and how far will this spread? And finally, what is the message that the prophets are trying to deliver?"

Why was he looking at *her*, Ziza wondered?

Lura made a loud huffing noise. "And you're hoping we'll translate it for you?"

"Not hoping," Talcott said. "We *expect* a translation. Before these deaths spread wider."

"We're in the business of language preservation," Lura said, waving a bangled wrist in the air, as if searching for the word she wanted. "Not sorcery. Languages are going extinct on a daily basis. It is all we can manage to preserve and record what we have. Nor is it likely that any new languages will spring up overnight."

"There's the Omega dialect from the Uminoya family," Dr. Renato suggested quietly, trying unsuccessfully to hide the grin tugging at his lips.

"The tribe that speaks Umi-omega doesn't technically count," Doctor Inez said. "Their language isn't new. We didn't know it existed until the late 'forties. We didn't know *they* existed."

Renato merely chuckled.

"The rest of the world knows very little about the old ways," Ziza said, her voice small but steady. What the scientists called "Umi-omega" was the language of Mãe's tribe.

Lura snorted. "What does that have to do with anything? We may be interested in the languages of the Uminoya but certainly not the witchcraft of your Mundomba."

"Not necessarily," Renato said. "Umi-omega seems oddly drawn to the Mundomba belief system. No one knows how long either of them have been in existence."

"Perhaps you could tell us," Doctor Inez said in her gentle voice, studying Ziza with her soft brown eyes. *It's okay*, those eyes told her.

"Since before Mãe's mother's time," Ziza said.

"Oh, that narrows it down," said Lura.

Ziza clamped her mouth shut. And they certainly weren't *her* Mundomba, despite the parasite within her.

Talcott cleared his throat and raised his voice to be heard over the murmur of private conversations rippling round the conference table. "Up until now we have only had personal accounts and sporadic digital captures that have given us information about the first sixteen cases. But now, for the first time, we have a recording that actually documents the verbal message." He nodded at Doctor Inez, who tapped in a code on her datapad. "You can listen to it for yourselves."

A voice floated out of the wallscreen, and Ziza sucked in her breath. It was Mãe's raspy voice from that night Ziza's mother channeled the spirits for the last time. It was the recording Ziza had handed over to Doctor Inez. "We are Tititri," Ziza's mother gasped. "We come." What was the mystery, Ziza wondered? Several of the linguists in the room understood her native dialect, Umi-omega, so what needed translating? Mãe clearly said what she said about the Tititri, whoever they were. Although, Ziza admitted, it was in another woman's voice, a lower and huskier voice than Mãe's. Different, because that was the spirit her mother channeled. In the recording, Mãe spoke Umi-omega, as always. She didn't speak some tribal language yet to be discovered and translated.

Then Mãe went on. "We help you die," Mãe said in the spirit's throaty voice. "You die next." Ziza didn't remember having heard any more words from her mother that night she died. How much of the night had Ziza lost? And where had the lost time gone? To the parasite, which had crept inside her, devouring her memory of that night. She shivered.

Ziza didn't want to die.

The linguists around the table shook their heads. "It's nothing recognizable," Lura said. "It's gibberish."

"Well, it's certainly not from the Uminoya family," said Renato.

"Nor the Tupi," Doctor Inez said.

"Then, none of you recognizes this language?" Talcott asked.

Doctor Inez nudged Ziza. "Go on," she said in that soft voice. "Tell them what you told me. You understand it."

What did they mean, Ziza wondered? She lurched forward in her seat and cried out. "But, it has to be Umi-omega. Why don't you know what she's saying? 'We are Tititri.' Can't you hear her?"

"We hear her," Doctor Inez said, "but we don't understand the words. She's not speaking any dialect of Uminoya that we know. No one but you seems to understand her."

Renato stroked his black and silver temples. "What is the element in common in their message that you mentioned?" he asked Talcott, but his gaze fixed on Ziza.

"Tititri," Talcott said. "Tititri is the one consistent sound that my contacts were able to replicate in their reports. And you clearly hear this woman say it, too. It's the rest of the message that we can't decipher."

Ziza's lower lip pushed out. What was happening? Were they playing games with her?

"Not just Tititri," Ziza shouted at them. "She also said 'we come'. And something about dying."

Did that mean that the Tititri — whoever they were — had already come? Because they must've killed Mãe when they invaded her spirit. Would they kill Ziza, too, through the parasite that wormed inside her?

# Chapter Six

WITH HIS TEA. WALKER SAT at the white, oval table in the seat indicated. H.F. Washington, the Director of the International Space Agency, was good at moving people around like pawns. H.F. greeted two more newcomers and seated everyone where he wanted them.

"We'll go ahead and begin," H.F. said, "even though we're waiting for one more." He assumed the head position, pulled up his fliptop data unit from the trap in the table, and invited the others to do the same.

Walker's preliminary report on the tachyonic emission came up first on the screen. He leaned back in his chair, crossed his arms, and watched the others study the specifics about the burst of tachyons he'd collected. H.F. peered intently at his readout, but Walker knew him well enough to recognize the pretense. The old man's arms dipped under the table where he would be fingering his string of beads. An indication, Walker worried, that this emission was bigger than any of them suspected. Too big, perhaps, for this assembly of top minds.

Margot Brandt, solar astronomer from the Mercury Station, frowned at the data on her fliptop, producing more wrinkles on an already leathery face.

Sitting across from Walker, a mirthless woman, Joy Masambwa, narrowed her black eyes to slashes as she studied her screen. Walker had heard of her — the renowned commander of the Jupiter Project. Although she was supposed to be Afran, she didn't appear to have a drop of black pigmentation in her skin. She favored black, devoid of color and warmth, in her shapeless work coveralls and the butchered style of artificially black hair. Walker wondered what she was doing here and how she fit into this "emergency." He hoped it didn't have to do with H.F.'s aliens. Walker didn't like the idea of public embarrassment for the old man.

"No," Dr. Brandt said, rapping a finger against her unit and pushing away from the table. A stringy tail of bleached blonde hair, yellowing badly, brushed her shoulders. "It cannot be. This emission does not conform to the model we usually see for solar activity. It might be originating from a planet, possibly one orbiting the principle pair of Alpha Centauri." She sighed heavily, apparently unhappy with her conclusion. Dark rings of sweat stained the underarms of her tunic. "Hell, we can't even tell if this emission is coming from the Centauri system or a point well beyond — "

"Yes, we can tell," Walker said softly. "My instruments have the capability to make that determination." Assuming they weren't broken, he thought. So far, diagnostics hadn't found any malfunctions.

Brandt snorted and flipped her fingers against her data unit. "You have, perhaps, substantiation from the results of your *machine*?" The way she mimicked him made his tachcom sound like a toy.

Walker didn't give her the satisfaction of an answer but instead returned her stare with equal intensity. With his arms folded, he pinched his fingers into his triceps and waited for someone else to crack under the strained air of the conference room.

H.F. took over. "What we definitely have is an anomaly," he said. "Something is emitting a patterned burst of tachyons, and it happens to coincide with other interesting events. Landon is best qualified to explain the pattern to us."

"What other events?" Walker asked.

"In time, my boy," H.F. said. "We will have to wait for Dr. Pereira to arrive before we get into that. Meanwhile, we are waiting to hear your interpretation."

Walker shifted in his seat, the back gummy from his sweat. "The burst we collected does show a pattern," he mumbled, pulling the stir stick from his tea. "It's similar to what we see when we're transmitting over the tachcom. My conclusion, if you've read that far, is that this is most likely a reflection of my lab's tachyonic work in communications over the years."

He wasn't sure Brandt had heard him. Twisting in her seat, she draped one arm across the back of her chair and appeared lost in thought, as if she'd mentally drifted away from Goiás. He felt Masambwa's gaze bore into him, and he knew she, at least, realized the significance of what he'd reported. His instruments were no toys.

Brandt returned her attention to the room and leaned forward against the table. "I'll tell you what. The Centaurus system is not a promising place for life to develop."

Here it came, Walker thought. "No one has mentioned anything about life," he said.

"No one had to," Brandt said. "It's obvious that's what this is all about, the way H.F. rushed us here, hush-hush."

"You're jumping to conclusions, doctor," Walker said.

"I think not. What you're really hinting at is a linguistic pattern to this tachyonic emission. Ergo, we're talking about an intelligence that produced the emission. Life."

Walker rubbed the back of his neck and wished it hadn't come to this. "You're looking at the wrong explanation. As I've said, tachyons exist everywhere in the universe. Just because we found a concentrated burst of them, originating from somewhere in the Centauri system, and just because their pattern is anomalous from what we would expect, doesn't mean it's caused by any extraterrestrials trying to communicate with us."

H.F.'s brows knitted together. "Can you rule out the possibility that this emission may be of alien origin?"

"Yes!" The word exploded from Walker. The director was always dim about this pet quirk of his. "The Drake equation clearly shows the unlikelihood of other intelligent life in the universe coinciding — "

"Only with pessimistic values plugged into your formula," H.F. said.

"Coinciding with ours," Walker continued, "on the same technological scale and within our reach during our lifetimes."

"I have to agree with Dr. Walker," Brandt said. "We can't be talking about any form of life, at least not one we can understand, and certainly not intelligent, not if its source is from a pair of dueling stars." She turned to H.F. "Now, what about those 'other events' you mentioned?"

Walker tensed, eager to learn the rest but dreading it at the same time. H.F. should've retired long ago. Pity to see such a brilliant man make a fool of himself.

"As Landon has pointed out," the director said, "his lab is the only one that has collected the signal."

Walker winced under the blow. "No, what you're not understanding is that this is an emission, not a signal. Signals are intentional, not random events. Regardless of what this is — a reflection or a random event — the significance is that we were able to pick it up. It's a good stream, and it's only a matter of time before other labs start to collect it, too."

"I'm sure, my boy," H.F. said. "You are the expert in this matter. I have complete confidence that you will interpret the signal for us. Now, let us skip ahead to the next item on the agenda." He tapped instructions into his data unit, and the promised report from Port Lowell appeared on their screens.

Walker scanned it quickly, feeling his nerves tighten, hearing gasps around the table, while everyone read about the accident.

H.F. cleared his throat, then spoke in a heavy voice. "As you can see, ladies and gentleman, we've lost the Valles Marineris Station. It was ISA's newest habitat, intended to become a major outpost for all branches of scientific study. It was still under construction on Mars when it exploded, otherwise the loss of life would've been much higher. All further development has been halted, pending an investigation."

"This sounds like the work of the Savers," Brandt muttered.

"No," said H.F. "They can't penetrate Mars."

Don't be so sure they wouldn't find a way, Walker thought. Terrorism was a more sensible explanation than a mistake on the part of H.F.'s engineers. He would've employed only the best.

Finally, Masambwa spoke. "And the relevance?" The famous commander apparently lacked a drop of warmth in her veins, judging from her icy demeanor. Walker suppressed a shiver.

"Look at the time, my dear," H.F. said.

"So?" Masambwa aimed the slashes of her coal-black eyes at him. Walker suspected that H.F. was the only person who could get away with calling the commander his "dear."

"It coincides with the time that Landon's lab intercepted the tachyonic emission," H.F. said.

Masambwa, sitting as if a board kept her rigidly upright, ignored that. "I repeat: explain to me the relevance of this unfortunate accident."

"What they're suggesting," Brandt said, trying unsuccessfully to hide her amusement, "is that tachyons destroyed the habitat."

"Nonsense!" Walker rapped his stir stick against the table. "Tachyons are subatomic particles that naturally occur in the universe. The difficulty in using them is their capture, as they stream through solid objects. No way they'd cause a structure like that to rupture. Something else — someone — had to be responsible for an explosion." He glanced at the others calmly watching his outburst. That was elemental, and they all knew such basics. "It had to be Savers, most likely."

"Not Savers," H.F. said.

"Then what's your answer? See here, H.F., what are you getting at?"

"Ladies and gentleman," H.F. began slowly, "you are correct to assume that I've summoned all of you here for a purpose beyond what you see in the data. The data simply serve to point to our purpose. We will change forever the future of our universe. We have the potential to save mankind from its inevitable destruction, but we are fast running out of time to do so." He paused, studying the three faces watching him. "I suggest we take a break and resume once Dr. Pereira is able to join us."

# Chapter Seven

GREER WALKER CAMERON hadn't asked for this. But what else could she do? The poor little baby, howling her lungs out. She was Greer's niece.

How much would that baby cost her?

Never mind, there was the court order. Greer could either comply, or she could join her flaky ex-sister-in-law in Patagonia.

But seriously, what else could Greer do but take in her own niece? As Aunt Jewel had done for her after Daddy's death.

But that was different. Times were different then, too. Back then, people had a choice — mostly — about where they wanted to live and who they wanted to live with. Now they had the world court telling them what to do. Force-draining bank accounts. Interrupting beauty treatments.

Greer intended never to grow old, not the way Aunt Jewel had.

But now. Now that the world court had yanked Greer out of her cryo-treatment, she was forced into attentiveness, and that meant — big sigh — aging.

Greer never was very good at following orders. That's why she'd immigrated here to the Holland Annex along with other free spirits when the opportunity arose some twenty-odd years ago.

Wait. She was only twenty-nine now, right?

She giggled.

But this time was different. She had no choice this time. If she didn't obey, she could lose everything. The trust fund Aunt Jewel had set up for her, and all the parties that came along with it. And besides, the poor little thing was her niece.

But she wished to hell the baby would shut the fuck up with that crying stuff.

What should Greer do? She'd never been around babies before. And that social service guy had only lingered long enough to install the sleeping baby in a crib and dump a box of basic care stuff. Was she expected to know how to use it?

"Don't worry," he'd said. "Mothering comes naturally."

Like hell, it did.

But really, what should she do? Why wouldn't the baby shut up? Landie had never made so much noise in his entire life. How could he possibly father such a set of lungs?

Okay. Maybe something was wrong. Even here in the Annex there were all kinds of bugs she knew not what. Maybe one of those had stung the baby or something. Maybe Greer should look.

Greer opened the door only a bare crack to peek into the guest room. The baby was standing up in the crib. Her face, swollen and red from crying, and her cheeks, shiny with tears. Her arms outstretched and her tiny fingers pumped.

Greer crept inside. "So," she said, swallowing hard. "Molilia. It's about time you and I met. Looks like we've only got each other now."

To Greer's surprise, the baby stopped crying. As if she'd understood and accepted the situation, which was more than Greer had done. The baby with a name longer than she was tall inserted her thumb in her mouth and looked Greer up and down.

"I know, I know," Greer said. "I must look like shit. I can't help it. I had to rush the treatment. I've got an appointment for a make-over later this week, and we're going to have to find something to do with you in the meanwhile. I'll tell you this: I don't intend to make any sacrifices, y'know, just because you've come to live here. So get used to it. Do that, and we'll get along just fine."

Molilia's thumb fell from her mouth as her face twisted into a fresh set of crying. Damn, Greer was going to have to watch what she said in front of her. You'd think the baby had actually understood her.

Well, why not? She wasn't stupid, after all. She probably got all of Landie's smart genes.

Just then the door buzzer rang. Greer stiffened. She wasn't expecting anyone. Molilia paused to listen, too. When Greer rushed out of the room, the baby burst out crying again. This time, Greer thought, her crying was more for show than sympathy.

Greer ignored the baby and switched on House for a view of her visitor. The woman in the entry far below looked vaguely familiar. Maybe it was just her perfect body that made Greer choke with envy. The woman must've had a body sculpt treatment. No one came like that naturally, with perfect distribution to her curves. Her suit showed off her curves, like an iridescent second skin that shimmered with each shift of her impatient movements. Her red and black hair showed money and pomp and style, slashed artistically and woven with sparkling adornments.

"Yes?" Greer said through House. She tried not to slip and let her excitement show over having such an obviously important visitor.

"Good evening. I'm Stephia Drummond with Worlds News Watch. Mind if I come up?"

So that's where Greer had seen her before. On the holo news. She quivered with anticipation as House guided her visitor to Greer's front door. What could such an important reporter want with *her*? She couldn't help feeling slightly suspicious, so she told House to remain on standby in case she needed its support. And meanwhile, suggest a suitable libation from Greer's inventory.

House chose a tawny port and had it ready and dispensed by the time Stephia arrived. Already on a first-name basis, they sank into the cushions of her sitting room. House had managed to mute Molilia's crying to a distant background sob.

Stephia tilted one ear up to the sound. "Yours?" she said, and then sipped her port.

"Um, sort of. That is, yes." Greer felt her heart swell. She hadn't expected that sudden rush of pride, and it left her confused and light-headed.

"I'll get to the point, then, since you're obviously busy. I'm doing a feature on the Savers. You've heard of them?"

"Who hasn't?" Greer snapped back. She might've recently come out of cryo-treatment, but she didn't live in a cave.

Stephia ignored her protest and went on. "It's time to expose the truth about the Savers. We always thought they were just another mixed-up doomsday group, thinking they could save the earth by destroying technology — "

"But they're not? Look, what've they got to do with me?" Greer bit her tongue, but the words were already out. Of course Stephia would know about Summer, Greer's flaky ex-sister-in-law.

"They think that the presence of our technology is a beacon in space," Stephia said with a trace of a smile, "and eventually it will draw aliens to us like a moth to flame. We'll all die then. Their arrival will trigger massive ecological upheaval. Doomsday."

"But technology is what's helping extend our lives," Greer said, a little confused. Or maybe a lot. The port wasn't helping matters.

"Technology doesn't have to extend our lives, say the Savers. They know of natural ways of healing, which are far safer than the risk of attracting aliens to us. They believe that the shamans of the world can assist with natural healing."

"Witch doctors, you mean?" Well, Summer was no witch, at least not that Greer knew of. Witchy, maybe. Definitely bitchy.

"If you like," Stephia said. "The point is that their spiritual systems show up in different variations around the world, but what they have in common is their connection to that intangible, immeasurable aspect of spirits."

"I've lost your point." Greer sipped her port.

Stephia sighed. "It's happening."

"You mean, aliens *are* coming?" Greer's heart rate picked up.

"Who knows?" Stephia said. "What we do know is what some of our investigative reporters at Worlds News Watch have discovered: shamans are dying around the world."

"That's a shame."

"You're not kidding, honey. And I think your brother knows more than he's telling about it."

"Landie? Oh, I get it. You think that just because his ex-wife is one of them, that he... Is that what you think?"

"I think he knows why the shamans are dying."

"He does?"

"It's all very hush-hush, of course. There are even rumors that the Savers have lost power. The public has a right to know what the shamans know, and it has to do with why they're dying. You could help."

"Me?"

"I understand your brother will be here soon."

"He will?"

"And when he comes, perhaps you could arrange an interview for me with him."

"You don't understand. Landie's not the interviewing type."

"Look, I always get my story in the end. I don't care if it's the end of the fucking world as long as I get the exclusive. You don't believe me? This is a matter of grave urgency, honey."

Greer's eyes popped open wide. "It's the end of the world?"

"Our mission at Worlds News Watch is to make certain the public stays informed. We cannot tolerate a conspiracy of cover-ups."

"A conspiracy? And ISA is involved? They're covering up the end of the world?"

Stephia shrugged. "Maybe it's what the Savers have always feared."

"Aliens?" Greer sputtered. "That's what they're afraid of. You said so yourself."

"We don't know exactly. That's why we need to talk to someone who does know."

"But Landie wouldn't know anything."

"He has access to information about the Savers."

"You think...that he thinks...that what the Savers think... You think they're right? Aliens are invading? Omigod!" Greer could see it now in her head, pictures of masses of panic-stricken people running in the streets, not knowing where they were running to, just running.

"Do you see the urgency of our situation?"

If it was true, Greer thought, that aliens were invading... If it was true that her brother knew about it... That would explain a lot. His rush to send Molilia to safety. Here. With Greer.

"Will you cooperate?" Stephia cocked her head, looking as if she tried to read Greer's thoughts, which only made Greer see how invasive the reporter really was. "Will you help me uncover the truth about the Savers?"

"The truth?" Greer wasn't sure what was true anymore.

Stephia sighed. "Why is your brother protecting the Savers?"

"You're wrong! Landie's not like that. You don't know him."

"Do *you*? What do you really know about your brother? And his child?"

"I know enough to know he'd never go along with a bunch of crackpots like the Savers."

"We'll pay you, of course."

So that was it. Well, she and Landie may have their differences, but she'd never — never! — betray her own brother. Still... "Exactly how much money are we talking about?"

# Chapter Eight

H.F. HAD ALWAYS BEEN A SHOWMAN, Walker thought, watching the old man lumber out of the room during the break. Even if his step had slowed, his passion and drama had not. It was so typical of H.F. to say things like that, promising to change the future of the universe. Saving mankind from destruction.

Sure. Walker remembered the first time he'd seen H.F.'s performance, when the director had been a guest speaker for Walker's graduate class at the University of British Columbia. H.F. had charged the entire class with his promises and dreams, and he'd infected Walker with hope. After that, nothing had ever been the same again for Walker.

Walker remained behind alone in the conference room, but the door stood open to the hall. Out there, footsteps clicked to and from the washroom. Then a man in a white suit appeared in the doorway and poked his head into the conference room. Badly in need of a haircut, he nodded a greeting at Walker. Then someone pulled the newcomer back into the hall.

Through the doorway, Walker saw a cluster of people, their backs turned to Walker.

"Commander!" the man in the white suit said. "Good to see you again."

"Likewise," Masambwa said in her monotone. "Recovered, I presume?"

"That's why I'm here," said the newcomer. Then with a chuckle, he added, "They can keep me from flying, but they can't keep me down."

H.F. returned from his trip down the hall and draped his arm around the shoulders of the man in the white suit. "I see everyone has met my new sidekick, Sam Talcott. And you've released our fine Dr. Pereira, so that she can now join us for the rest of this discussion? Sorry, Sam, this meeting isn't for you, not until your probationary status rolls over. A nuisance, I know, but have patience. We have to put up with procedure."

"No problem," said Talcott. "I've got plenty of paperwork to fill out."

He seemed an amiable fellow, Walker thought, watching Talcott wave and continue down the hall, but he'd never known H.F. to have a "sidekick." H.F. looked even more tired as he ushered the others back into the conference room. It was about time H.F. took on more help. Yes, Sam could be a godsend.

H.F. introduced the linguist, Dr. Inez Pereira, and directed her where to sit at the table. He reseated himself and then took a long, dramatic sip of his drink. Apparently satisfied that he held everyone's attention, he continued as if there'd been no break at all. "From the actual sequence of the signal itself, Dr. Pereira has determined a certain, shall we say, linguistic pattern to the data."

"I thought so," Brandt said. "Didn't I tell you?"

"Of course it is," Walker said, "at least partially. Some of my tests have attached oral transmissions. After all, that's the point of instantaneous communication."

"But how is that possible," Brandt asked, "when everyone knows that given their faster-than-light properties, tachyons travel through time?"

"Time travel is actually what's happening," Walker said, "but I only see my beam of tachyons as the carrier. Then I aim it to arrive at a pre-calculated coordinate that coincides with the position of my receiver in order to effect instantaneous communication. You could use it for the past or the future, but that's not my work. I'll leave that to Van Pelt. He's doing excellent, theoretical work in that area over in the Holland Annex, although he hasn't actually achieved it. As I've already mentioned, this emission, the one we're talking about, is significant because it's merely a reflection of my work. An echo."

Pereira shook her head. "No, actually it's not. The patterns indicate a new language, something that's never been known before on Earth."

"That's complete guesswork." Walker had known it. The linguist was a quack. "We don't have the full burst. By the time those particles reach us, they're drifting away from the main stream of them. We can try feeding what we have into the converter, but any results you get will be false. The data are incomplete. You can't assume — "

"All right, all right." H.F. thrust his hands up from beneath the table, then pounded one of them against its surface. Amber beads rattled on the plastic. "I don't pretend to understand the process. But I'll tell you this. I respect the work of Dr. Pereira, as I respect each of yours. Maybe what we're seeing is a new language in this emission. Maybe it's something else. But we are reasonably certain that this is not a reflection of your work, Landon. Neither is the origin of this signal a random, naturally occurring event. It's deliberate, suggesting someone has to be responsible — "

The stir stick snapped in Walker's fingers.

H.F. smiled faintly at the broken pieces in Walker's hand and continued. "We have reason to believe that this message is intended for Earth. It's aimed directly here. It passed through Mars, which is presently in alignment between Earth and the Centauri system, it destroyed my habitat, and it showed up at your laboratory on SpaceHab."

"You need more than that to make such an assumption," Brandt said. "More than likely, we're only intercepting the emission. It might truly be 'aimed' at a point beyond us."

"You're not telling us anything we don't already know," Walker said quietly. "What *aren't* you telling us?"

H.F. gave Walker a sour look. "Dr. Pereira believes she's found a translation of the message."

Walker's head throbbed. "How is that possible? If indeed this is an alien language, then what's the connection between that and one of Earth's? What's the Rosetta Stone?" He regretted the question as soon as he'd uttered the words, for it sounded as if he was accepting H.F.'s premise.

H.F. took in a large breath, huffing up his chest. "You can now read a portion of the message, translated on your screens."

*We are Tititri... We come... You die next.*

Walker blinked. The room swayed around him. He read again. The words didn't change.

*Tititri... Tititri...* Where had he heard that before? *Die?*

"Tititri?" Brandt stumbled over the name. "Who or what the hell's that?"

"Who they are," H.F. said, "we don't know. Perhaps they're the builders of the Titan ruins. Or perhaps they're the enemies who forced the Titan builders to abandon Titan. Why the Tititri have chosen us as their target, we don't know. We have to find out, because their intentions definitely don't appear friendly."

"Shit! They want to kill us?" Brandt sputtered.

H.F. paused and looked at Masambwa. "As for the relevance that you were asking about, Commander: our loss of the Valles Marineris station indicates the Tititri's hostility. Whatever their intentions are, it's already begun. But we're not going to sit here and wait for them to test how brave we are. The only way we can take control of the situation and find out what they want from us is by going there ourselves."

Brandt sucked in her breath. "Go *where*, exactly?"

Pereira's eyebrows arched.

"Ladies and gentleman," H.F. continued, "ISA has just authorized its first manned mission to another star. Joy Masambwa, who believes her ship from the Jupiter Project can be outfitted for interstellar travel, will be its commander." He nodded at the cold woman, giving her a cue.

"We mined sufficient helium-3 from the Jovian atmosphere to fuel a mission of this sort, gentlemen," Masambwa said. Brandt and Pereira exchanged glances. "We can get to the Centauri system and back, but I don't recommend it. Not yet. We shouldn't begin to undertake a mission of that magnitude for two or three more years, at least. Not until we harvest a larger supply of fuel to allow for any unknowns we might encounter along the way."

"You don't need it," H.F. said, "because we don't have the advantage of time. We've scheduled four months to pull this mission together. That's all the time you've got to acquire additional reserves."

"It won't be enough. In my opinion, sir."

"Yet, it is the opinion of Oswald's group in the Annex that we presently have sufficient reserves, not only for the trip but also for an emergency supply."

"Yes, sir, I'm familiar with that particular study." Masambwa clenched her jaw as if to bite off the words Walker thought she ought to say: Let Oswald command the mission.

"Are you uncomfortable operating under their recommendations?" H.F. was relentless when he wanted something.

"No sir, I am not."

"Very well, then. You will be ready to start training with the remainder of your crew next week."

"On one condition." She crossed her arms against her chest. As if this woman needed to steel herself.

H.F.'s bushy eyebrows shot up. His beads clinked onto the floor beneath the table. "And that is?"

"That I have final approval of crew selection."

H.F. sighed. "Naturally. But let me remind you, commander. If anybody's profile doesn't fit with the rest of the crew during preliminary testing, he or she is out."

"Naturally."

"I know all of you are tired from your long trips here," H.F. continued, "but I want to stress that we have no time to spare. Once we get this mission aloft, it'll take some twelve of our years before you reach the periphery of the Centauri system. Whatever message they're sending us will probably be gone by then, but — "

"Message, hell!" Brandt shouted. "Earth could be blown up by then if they're as hostile as you imply."

"We don't know yet what they want from us, Dr. Brandt." H.F. kept his voice low and smooth. "As I was saying, when you apply Landon's new work in trail analysis, I'm confident you'll find the source of the signal. And along with it, we'll have some answers. Then we'll know how to proceed."

"If we're still alive." Brandt slouched in her chair.

"Twenty-four of our years is nothing in terms of the universe," Pereira said.

"Wait a minute," Walker said, shaking his head. This discussion wasn't making sense. "What's this mission really about?"

"Quite simply," H.F. answered, lifting his shaggy eyebrows, "we're talking about a first contact. What could be more important? When we pull this off, ISA will be set in perpetuity."

"No, really," Walker said, clenching his fingers into a fist until his knuckles ached. Sure, H.F. had his obsessions, but he was far too astute to throw away a major chunk of his resources on...a *hoax*. He couldn't actually think he'd received a message from aliens. Aliens. Had the director lost his mind? The universe was nicely balanced, in Walker's opinion, without this unrealistic idea upsetting the equations that governed his life.

H.F. sighed. "All right, then, would you understand it better if I said it's about the future of Earth?"

Brandt huffed. "You want us to go to the Centaurus system to fight some...some, hell, I don't know...pissed-off Centaurians?"

"No, doctor," said H.F. "I want you to go there to identify the problem and then diffuse it. Before it's too late for us." The old man sighed and bent over, retrieving his beads from beneath the table. "Maybe it all ready is too late." Then he rose, signaling an end to the meeting. "I'll give each of you until morning to decide whether you're with us or not. Dr. Pereira will escort you to your guest quarters. We'll resume again at eight a.m. sharp to finalize crew selection." Then he gave Walker a pointed look. "Landon, I'm counting on your assistance."

Meaning, Walker thought, that he didn't have a decision to make. He was already on board whether or not he liked it.

He didn't like it.

"H.F.," Walker said, "I have to remind you that I have a daughter here on Earth. I can't just abandon her."

"You won't, my boy.  You and I will remain here directing operations."

So he wasn't going.  It was the answer he wanted, and yet... Walker balled his fist under the table.

# Chapter Nine

**W**ALKER WATCHED CLOSELY through his porthole as ISA's shearjet descended toward the North Sea. The watery surface looked ruffled even from this distance, and he wondered how the Annex's manmade walls could keep back that sea in a storm.

*Would Molly be safe growing up in such an environment?*

He stiffened, and a surge of anxiety pulsed through his veins. He'd assumed the bullet in Goiás had been an effort to sabotage H.F.'s plans, not a personal vendetta against Walker. Maybe he was wrong. If so, he could be leading an unknown enemy to his only family, just by coming here.

"Dr. Walker, prepare for landing," came a mechanical voice at his back.

He pulled away from the window. He was the only passenger in this sleek twelve-seater. A steward bot stood blinking at the side of his seat, waiting while Walker's chair activated and swiveled into locked position. Then the transparent shield slid out from one side, sealing him into his own safety pod. Satisfied, the bot rolled away, securing and retracting data and entertainment units that had been set up for Walker's sole use.

He was grateful for the solitude. In this type of craft, he didn't even have to see the pilots. This was H.F.'s doing, sending him on the shear with a bot instead of a human server. H.F. understood Walker's need to be alone.

Within his pod, he flipped on the screen, which gave him the pilots' view of landing. Not all passengers had the stomach to watch this, but it was child's play compared to the last time he'd touched down to Earth. The shear's course paralleled the straight coast, an uninteresting flatland broken occasionally by fingers of oozing sea. Then it was a quick hop across open sea to the floating landing strip that served the man-made island habitats. Collectively known as the Holland Annex, this place helped boost the Dutch economy along with a flood of immigrants, like Walker's kid sister, Greer. Best as he could tell, she did nothing, unlike the other immigrants who'd brought with them the newest enterprises and laboratories on the cutting edge of science and technology.

He switched off the screen and closed his eyes, feeling the smooth, dipping movement of the shear. Yes, he could understand the lure of a place like this, even for his sister. New places were always exciting for their potential. The Annex was a city without the baggage of history. It offered a second chance for a more sane and rational life in a new community. It was a place like SpaceHab or any community in space that, unlike Earth, promised a future.

But Greer couldn't see the similarity.

———

WALKER FOUND HIS SISTER WAITING for him when he emerged from Customs. The first thing he noticed was that she was alone. For an instant, disappointment choked him. Then he pushed it off and felt his blood pressure rise — she'd left Molly so soon? The social services agent had just turned over the child a few days ago. He took a deep breath and told himself that Greer would make sure the baby was safe.

She was sensible enough, even if she never looked it. The second thing he noticed about her was her hair — dyed-black, close-cropped with patterns of a mermaid shaved into it. She was always following current fads, much to his distaste.

"Landie!" she cried, using the pet name that sent chills up Walker's spine. She pushed through a milling crowd and launched herself into his arms.

He stood his ground and managed to retain his grasp on his carryall. "Good to see you, Greer," he said, staring at the intricate waves of white scalp.

"You haven't changed at all," she said.

He could almost feel her probing eyes on him, and he let his gaze wander across her face, decorated with glittery designs he couldn't decipher. "That's not true, of course. It's been, what? Ten years? I've added some gray and a few pounds."

Releasing him, she arranged her face into a pout, but when she smiled again, not a hint of a wrinkle showed amidst the sparkles painted on her skin. Odd, he thought. She was definitely past forty, although he couldn't pinpoint the year, but the elasticity of her skin made her look far younger. Cosmetic treatments, no doubt. He envisioned Molly's upbringing with misplaced emphasis on vanity over scholarship, whimsy over discipline, and shivered.

What other choice had there been? The courts decided for them.

Greer led him out into the thin, August sunshine and summoned her car. It was bug-small, bright yellow, and solar-silent. He flung his bag into the rear luggage rack, then folded himself into the passenger seat. Greer slid in behind the wheel, told it "Home," then leaned back and evaluated him through slits of gray eyes.

"I wanted a chance to talk to you first, before Molilia takes all your attention," she said as the car merged into a stream of traffic heading up an elevated byway. "And where on earth did you come up with such a cool name? That's so not like you."

"Not my idea. I call her Molly."

"Summer named her? Well, she's right, this time. Molilia is better. I'm not complaining about taking care of her. I understand why the courts brought her to me, since I'm all the family she's got left. Poor little thing, losing her mother. And you and your precious work. But you need to realize that I'm not going to give up my life for her. Neither one of us has to give up anything for the other."

"What are you trying to say?"

She laughed. "Still the same old Landie, aren't you? What I'm trying to tell you is that two people can live together, grow together without stifling each other. One of them doesn't have to give up her life for the other."

"Look, Greer, don't blame me for putting Molly into cryo-sleep. There was no room for her in the nursery when…I needed it all of a sudden…because Summer…" His voice faltered, and he quickly added, "It was either that, or give up my work."

"I know, I know. Your precious work."

"At least I have something meaningful to do with my life." He focused on the organized chaos of traffic streaming in every direction.

"And so have I, Landie, even if you don't recognize it as important. I'm carrying on the legacy for Aunt Jewel."

He snorted. Jewel Cameron wasn't even their biological aunt, although she *had* taken Greer in after their father's death. Their mother had disappeared long before that, somewhere into the rehab system. Anger simmered through him. Between his crazy mother and crazy ex-wife, what were Molly's chances? How defective were Molly's genes?

"Don't scoff, Landie. Aunt Jewel was one woman who knew how to live life to its fullest. I intend to continue in that tradition."

"Improving on tradition is even better. Greer, there's something I want you to do for Molly."

"You know I'll do anything for her. Within reason, of course."

"Get a DNA analysis on her." He watched the facial designs fire on his sister's cheeks in the glow of a setting sun.

"But she already had one at birth. Why another one?"

"The birth registry only does a basic. I want a full work-up."

"Don't tell me you're worried *now* about what the tank did to her?"

"Of course not. The tank can't change a person's genetic makeup. Besides, tanks are perfectly safe these days. Do you think I ever would've considered it, otherwise?" His eyebrow twitched.

"Ah, I get it. You want to make sure she doesn't have whatever it is that made Summer go mad. That's it, isn't it?"

He frowned. "I just thought it'd be a good idea. To know. That's all."

Her voice softened. "How *is* Summer, anyway?"

He shrugged. How would he know? The Patagonian Penitentiary was no holiday, but Summer deserved the maximum facility after trying to blow up SpaceHab. He could feel the veins standing out on his temples.

Greer reached across the cramped space of the car and patted his knee. "You won't have to worry about Molilia. I'll give her a stable home while you go hide in your laboratory and do what you have to do. I know how important stability is to you."

He ignored the liberal dose of sarcasm in her tone and nodded, turning to stare at the tiered landscape of buildings, reflecting golden light. "While I'm here, we'll open a fund which you can access for her care."

Greer let out a shrill whistle, which turned his attention away from the tinted glass and steel structures and back onto her agitation. "Do you realize how much it's going to take to raise her properly?"

He thought. "I guess not. Maybe I should transfer more. I won't need much. Only pocket change in Goiás."

"You don't get it, do you?" She shook her head, but the mermaid design didn't fluff. "Do you think handing over your salary to her will make up for disappearing from her life?"

"I'm not disappearing, Greer, and she's only a year old." The headache surfaced into a hammering rhythm, and his drugs were out of reach, in his bag.

She cocked her head at him. "Don't you know your own daughter's birthday? She's seventeen months."

He flushed, rejecting the reminder of those lost months, and quickly turned away.

"What matters," she continued to his back, "is that Molilia is a little girl, and she's going to grow up alone. Without her parents."

"She has you. She'll think you're her mother."

Greer's voice took on a rough edge. "A girl needs a father. I should know that well enough."

"Molly has one," he mumbled. *Even though I had no say in the matter.* Summer had gone off her pill and then forged the necessary documents to access his sperm bank at the fertility center while he was away on Mars. But once the baby was born, Summer never bonded with her. Summer ended up rejecting the child to join that cult that brainwashed her into dressing up as a suicide bomber. Greer didn't know the bloody details, and he preferred to keep it that way.

"You men are all alike. Your brains are in your penis. You think that's all there is to it?"

Whipping around to face her, he felt the heat rise from him. "What do you expect of me?"

"To be her father. To show some fatherly responsibility."

"Setting up an account for her is not fulfilling my responsibility to her?" He scowled at the smug smile on her face — she was so certain that she had all the answers. Then he looked away to study the blurring scene they whizzed past.

The landscape had lost its glitter. Why did they use so much glass in a place like this, he wondered, a place vulnerable to the elements? Must be reinforced. Probably not glass at all. Maybe this city wasn't what it appeared, either.

"I'm not talking about financial responsibility," she continued. "Why do you have to work so hard? Why can't you make any time for your family?" Her voice rose to a whine of hysteria.

"Calm down, Greer. I'm here, aren't I? Besides, I can't quit now. That's impossible." She reminded him of Summer, the way she kept niggling him without saying what was on her mind. He'd had to learn how to control his temper, to suppress the angry piranhas always lurking beneath the surface of civility. The only times he'd ever let them loose had been with the women in his life. Now he took a deep breath in an effort to keep his irritation at bay. "I can't give up my work because of a child."

"But this isn't any child we're talking about." Greer punched him on the arm, which got his immediate attention. "Landie, Landie, let's not fight. Maybe it's a good thing we don't see each other so often. I'll do what I can for Molilia, but I want you to know you're making a big mistake. I want you to consider the consequences of your career path. You're going to miss out on your child's life. Both of you are going to suffer dreadfully before this is over. I know that has to matter to you. Otherwise, you wouldn't be here. You wouldn't have come, just to set up a bank account when you could've handled that over the net."

"I'm here to escort a mission member back to Goiás."

She laughed outright. "And this person is unable to find his or her own way there?"

"Once they start training next week, there won't be another opportunity for me to get away to come here." He scowled. Had she thought he could immerse himself in work without saying good-bye first? "Maybe I can arrange guest quarters for you and Molly to spend some time in Goiás, instead."

"You're afraid of what you might find, and you're too proud to admit it."

He wanted to protest, but if he let her probe too far, she might find out things she didn't need to know. Things that would worry her too much.

"Well, if you're not afraid, I am." Her voice trembled in the gulf of silence between them, and she reached for his hand. "Quit, Landie. You can find something here. The cost is just too high, working for that man, Washington."

"What do you know about cost?" he said, staring at her in the dimming interior of the car racing into twilight. He wondered if she'd blown through all of Jewel Cameron's inheritance by now.

"Nothing. It's just that... Oh, Landie, something bad's going to happen. They won't say in the news, but I can feel it coming."

"All you should worry about is your ocean. Oceans are rising."

"No, that's not it. Worse than that."

"What could be worse than global disaster?" If H.F. was right about the signal, the Tititri were sending warnings of death. Death for Earth, he thought with a shiver. "A place farther inland might be nice. The Alps, perhaps."

"We're safe enough here," she said. "The Annex rises with the water level, haven't you noticed?"

He shook off Greer's hand and looked away. Lights sparkled from the domes of this floating land. Whoever had dreamed up this place was either a visionary or an idiot. Same as H.F., for pulling together the Centauri mission.

"All I'm asking, Landie, is that you think about what you're doing."

"I've already given it enough thought."

"Have you, really? No, I don't think so."

"I have no choice."

"Yes, you do. Landie, you don't have to do everything that H.F. Washington wants, just because *he* asks you to."

"You don't understand —"

"That's so typical of you! You haven't heard a thing I've said! You haven't even said what this new project of his is about. Why it's so important. Why have *you* got to do it instead of someone else?"

He'd heard. "Greer... There are things about my work...that I'm not at liberty to tell you."

Her voice trembled. "Then that reporter was right. You *do* know!"

"What reporter? What are you talking about?"

"She wants to take us to dinner. Ask you a few questions."

"That's impossible! What have you told her?"

"Nothing, Landie. What do I know? Anyhow, what's so classified about what you're working on?"

He cleared his throat. "You can't talk to anyone. Promise me that."

"Okay, okay. Don't get all excited. But you could've told me, y'know. I can keep a secret, if that's what you want."

"When the time is right, H.F. will make a public announcement. Until then, just forget about what I might be doing."

"It's that bad, huh?" Her face screwed up with worry. "You're getting ready to leave again, aren't you? Are you going back to Mars? Or somewhere even farther?"

He'd already revealed too much, making her suspect that a mission was in the works. But he couldn't tell her anything, not even that he wasn't going away. If word about the emission leaked out to the general public, they'd think it was a signal, too, and it could start a general panic. Dead shamans were bad enough. They would be all the proof the media would need.

"I can tell you this much," Walker said. "Basically, I'm doing what I always do: provide support for instantaneous communication between extra planetary missions and Earth." It wasn't exactly a lie. It just wasn't the complete truth. The information that the crew members would have to relay using *Walker's* equipment, assessing the situation in the Centauri system, could be the critical piece of information they needed to save Earth from whatever threat H.F. thought was out there.

"There's more, isn't there?" Greer asked.

He was going to prove H.F. wrong. "Trust me," he whispered, as Dopplered whines of traffic zipped past them.

# Chapter Ten

WALKER DREAMED OF VOICES that night, disembodied voices chanting meaningless sounds in a wailing pitch... Moaning, crying, whispering voices, calling his name. "Lannnnnndonnnnn..." "Daaaa." Everyone needed him.

Walker's gut cramped. Something bound him, imprisoning him, the way the slim tanks for cryo-sleep clamped around a body.

Gradually, he became aware of a whistling, skittering sound. He was sweating beneath his twisted-up sheet. Then a flash strobed through his state of semi-consciousness, followed moments later by a loud boom. He opened his eyes to a flood of dark and breathed in thick air with a trace of salt. Jerking upright in the narrow bed in Greer's guest room, he wondered how he could sense the storm rolling across the city. His sister's apartment was on the sixth floor and deep within a dome cluster. Had she left the access to the outdoors *open*?

This was not the four o'clock shower at SpaceHab, programmed to cleanse the air. No, this was the real thing. He untangled himself from the sheet and swung his legs over the edge of the bed. Adrenaline raced through him, jolting him awake. Definitely not a gentle awakening from cryo-sleep.

The last time he'd experienced a real Earth storm had been ten years ago, when he and Summer had honeymooned in a Costa Rican villa.

The skittering noise repeated itself, and he got up and padded to the viewer in his bare feet. Something must be brushing against the exterior in the gale, and he could hear it through the access vents Greer was supposed to have closed. He wondered if the building strained under the pressures of the squall off the North Sea. In his underwear, he stood there, staring through the multi-panes of the false window, seeing nothing but kaleidoscopic shadows, shifting in shades of gray. He groped for the selector and switched to a sea view. Under the foggy glow of the city's nightlights, he could see the ghostly shapes of whitecaps lashing at the perimeters of the dome exterior. Was it his imagination, or could he feel the building swaying under his feet?

A whimper sounded from the other side of his bedroom door. Molly. He rubbed his temples and waited.

The whimpers grew stronger, reminding him of the way her cries had built that first night he'd spent alone with her — after the security officers had spotted Summer in her failed bomb suit and hauled her away, screaming and fighting until they'd had to sedate her. Then, Walker was the only one available to offer awkward comfort to the baby. But this time Greer would handle her. Where was she?

Listening for his sister's movements, he no longer heard the storm raging outside. He paced in the dark, bumping into unfamiliar pieces of furniture, as Molly's cries continued, gathering momentum. Covering his ears with his hands didn't make the sounds go away. It didn't bring Greer to his rescue, either. The cries grew more intense, piercing. His head throbbed.

Finally, he threw open his door and raced down the carpeted hall to the alcove where they'd moved the crib. The baby stood with her arms reaching up over the railing. Her feet danced as if she stood on a bed of hot coals.

"There, there," he murmured, lifting her up.

She burrowed her wet cheek against his neck and gurgled, swallowing her wails. Wispy curls snagged against the stubbles of his chin. Her little body heaved with spasms in the aftermath of sobs. Tiny fingernails clawed at him, nailing herself to him.

She'd probably never experienced a natural storm before, he realized, tightening his arms around the child. For once, his parental magic worked.

She let out a long, shuddering sigh and relaxed in his arms.  Something creaked, and he looked up in time to see Greer's bedroom door shutting.

"Molly," he whispered, pressing his face against his daughter's.  Tears formed a slippery seal between them.

# Chapter Eleven

I
T WAS STILL RAINING THE NEXT MORNING when he took Greer's car to the cryo-genics unit of the Rijnland Complex. The coordinates had already been entered in the car's memory, meaning that Greer had been there. Or at least the car had.

Rain-slickened high-rises of the city blurred past him. He kept won-dering what business Greer'd had with cryogenics. The way she'd protested Molly's insertion into cryo-sleep back on SpaceHab, he'd always assumed his sister disapproved of the concept. But considering her attraction to fads, that didn't make sense. More and more people — the wealthy, mostly — were opting for cryo-sleep as a trendy way to postpone whatever crises faced them. No, his sister didn't add up, and he experienced a moment of regret, realizing he didn't really know her at all.

The car stopped, surprising him that he'd already arrived. He stared through needling rain at a gray mausoleum of a building, then darted to its front door. Behind him, the car slid away to a parking slot. A retinal scan admitted him, and a mechanical mouse crawled out of a wall socket to direct him along the antiseptic corridors of the building. He shivered. The air felt extra chilly in these halls, but perhaps it was only because he knew that fro-zen humans lay on the other side of the walls.

*It wasn't so bad*, he told himself, shrugging off his uneasy feeling. They'd lost a few of the early cryonics experiments. Today the procedure's success rate was high enough to be considered safe.

He'd tried it himself, a few years back, while on the mission to Titan originally intended to test tachyons in that methane atmosphere. H.F. had recommended cryo-sleep for him. At his age, Walker shouldn't waste unnecessary aging time on travel. The most difficult part of the entire experience was when it was all over, and he returned to a world that had advanced beyond the scope of his knowledge. It had left him with an uncomfortable, out-of-sync feeling. Yes, it was safe, but he wouldn't want to use cryo-sleep any more than necessary.

On *this* journey, it would be necessary for all eight crew members.

The mouse stopped at the door to a cramped office, beeped, then inserted itself back into the wall. So this was the place, Walker thought, the site of the appointed meeting. He peered inside the closet-sized room. A desktop folded out of one wall and filled most of the area. Judging from the clutter atop the table's surface, it must remain in the down position permanently. The wall space behind it, where theoretically the desk would store itself, displayed awards in all sizes and shapes, some with holograms of distinguished groups of strangers whose eyes followed Walker's movement while he paced, waiting in the confined space. Fortunately, he didn't have to wait long. After a few moments, footsteps clicked down the hall, then a tall, slightly hunched woman in a rumpled lab coat strode inside.

She moved directly to Walker while extending her hand. "You're Landon," she said in a heavy, French accent. "I'm Renee Montague. Finally, we meet."

He hesitated longer than comfort allowed, then cleared his throat. "Dr. Montague," he said, stressing the title, as if that would restore a more formal distance between them. He took her hand, but as soon as he did, she slipped away, peeling off her coat and flinging it onto a hook behind the door. It hung in crooked folds, but she didn't take the time to straighten it.

"We should dispense with titles, don't you think?" she said, stepping out to face him again. Dark circles shadowed her eyes. Lines crinkled around the sharp, pinched features of her face and radiated away like tiny fractures to a bald scalp. Her slight shoulders drooped, as if the length of her arms, too long even for her stick-like height, weighed her down. It looked as if it required all of her strength to muster a smile of welcome.

"After all," she continued, ripping her Velcroed chart pad from a slim, almost anorexic waist, then adding it to the clutter on her desk, "we will be working together a long, long time. Take off your coat and have a seat. You're dripping on my papers." She looked around the floor space, littered with stacks of papers and crates of data sticks, and frowned as if she'd misplaced the chairs. Spying one that satisfied her, she scooped up the gadgets covering its cushioned seat and dropped them into a crate. "Something to drink?" she asked.

"No, thanks."

She sat down at her desk, then leaned across several stacked trays to touch a button on the protruding com screen. "Nora," she said, "two coffees. Make them black." Looking back at Walker, she grinned. "Doctor's orders. I've been up two nights in a row, working to get things ready."

*Great. A woman who doesn't listen.* He would speak to H.F. about her profile and whether or not it was the best fit for the mission.

She massaged her temples. "How much time do I have to finish getting ready?"

"The shearjet leaves tomorrow morning. I'll be round to pick you up at — "

"No, no," she said, waving at the pesky air in front of her nose. "We'll have to call H.F. and tell him we need more time."

Walker sagged deeper in his seat, feeling as if he'd been dealt a hammer blow from above. "How much more time do you need?" He'd already been away from his work three days. He couldn't afford to become too accustomed to his daughter.

Montague's shoulders lifted into a shrug, and the corners of her mouth turned down. "There is much still to be done, no?" She swept her arm in a wide arc, indicating the room and its spilled contents. "And I've been pulled away from all this with my new patient — that pilot from the Mars accident."

"If I help you, can you be ready by morning?"

She opened her eyes and smiled, bringing a glimmer of amusement to her weary demeanor. "Tell me, Landon. Are you in a rush to leave our fair Annex?"

"Not at all," he said, tugging his collar where he felt the heat from his lie building. He couldn't risk more memories like last night's storm and the soft feel of Molly's plump cheek against his neck. They would only complicate his purpose.

"H.F. is pushing the schedule," he said, feeling his way through the lame explanation. "That's all. Four months are not long to train for a mission of this nature. We can't afford a delay at this point. That's why I'm here. To see that there is none, to see that H.F.'s schedule is followed."

"Hmmm. He will not push it, I think, at the risk of a too hastily assembled cryogenics laboratory."

"Do you have an assistant you trust?" he asked. "Someone who can help speed things up?"

"Of course. But I must still be here to supervise. We are talking about the lives of eight human beings on this mission. Do you know what it is to be responsible for that?"

"I think so. I, too, am responsible for the people in my lab."

She chuckled. "It is not, I think, the same thing. No, not at all."

She was right, of course, and he squirmed, realizing this woman had the power to make him say stupid things. He wouldn't make his weakness worse, however, by backing down from her stare. When Nora entered, interrupting them, he sighed with relief. He might even drink the proffered coffee.

After the assistant left, Montague sniffed at her cup, then leaned back in her chair with a look of smug self-satisfaction. "Why did you say 'yes'?"

One of his eyebrows lifted inadvertently. "To what?"

She laughed, apparently not fooled. "To H.F., of course."

"Was there any other choice?"

She frowned, a woman of quick-change expression. "There is always a choice, and you have your family to consider. Of all of us, you are the only one with immediate family."

"Look," he said, trying to keep the sharp edge from his voice. "I'm not going, remember?"

"You are part of the team, no?"

"This is pointless. This isn't about me. You and I could better spend our time packing your supplies than talking about me. Let's get to work." He started to rise. The sooner he got her packing, the sooner he could search for Van Pelt's lab in one of the many buildings here. Walker had to find out why Van Pelt's equipment hadn't picked up this stream of tachyons as it should have.

"Sit." Montague scooted her chair forward and dropped her fingers down to drum her nails against the arm rests. Something in her manner made him obey. "I am not asking you these questions because I take sadistic pleasure in your clear discomfort. You must understand this. I am the medical doctor on this mission, and as such, it is imperative that I understand my patients, physically and emotionally. Now do not be insulted. Yes, yes, you are my patient, too, if you are on the team. You will be sequestered along with the rest of us for the next several months. It is my job to keep the team well, and I cannot perform my job if I do not understand your background, yes? Good, we understand each other."

She swiveled her chair over to the data unit, switched it on, then reached for one of the boxes of sticks. Walker wondered how she knew which one she wanted. But she must have a sense of order within the chaos of her office, for she removed a cartridge from the first box she touched, then popped it into the loader.

"*Voilà*," she said, studying the screen. "Landon Alfred Walker. Born in Vancouver, B.C. One sibling, Greer Allison Walker. You were raised by a single father, a sports announcer."

A corner of her mouth twitched as if she wanted to smile but fought it. His father's passion for sports had always produced that effect on Walker's more scholarly associates. Now, he sank lower into the chair cushion, feeling pummeled down as he watched Montague scroll through his life.

"Mother disappeared two months after sister's birth," she mumbled. "Turned up six years later in a drug treatment center. Then vanished again."

She took in a deep breath and turned with a question on her face, demanding a response, an explanation for the universal ineptitude that had caused a life to go awry, an unfixable life.

He shuddered, made a fist, and let it go. No point in fighting it now, he thought. The loss of his mother was part of the irretrievable past.

The woman focused on her screen again. "You had a childhood case of pneumonia despite your immunity series," she told him, tapping in notes to herself. "Any recurring respiratory problems?"

"No, of course not. That was a long time ago."

She studied her screen again and chewed on her lower lip. He watched her eye movement darting across the data and wondered which highlights she'd filed away in her mind. She would've already reviewed his background; why make him watch her drag it all across her screen?

"What's this black belt all about?" she asked suddenly, straightening in her seat.

"Dad and I trained together in an ancient sport — Tae Kwon Do. It strengthened my lungs and taught me the discipline I've needed to..."

She looked away from the screen and watched him. "Go on. The discipline you needed to do what?"

He cleared his throat. "To carry on with my work."

"I see."

She turned back to her review of his life, and he wondered if he'd convinced her. "Say, I thought when we're done here I'd look up Van Pelt. Do you know him?"

"This is a big place, and they don't let me out of this unit very often." She laughed, her voice a cackling sound.

He cradled his forehead with his fingertips as he listened to her steady typing of notes. Abruptly, the clicking sounds stopped. Something new had caught Montague's attention, and he looked up. She leaned closer to her screen, frowned, and shook her head. He could guess where she was in his life. She glanced over at him, as if for confirmation, and the tiny creases on her face softened into sympathy lines. He didn't need her sympathy. He looked away, intently studying the holograms of strangers decorating Montague's awards.

*One of the Savers' bombs destroyed the Vancouver SportDome. Along with Dad.*

But Montague didn't dwell on it. At least he would give her the credit for realizing it was better to go on than look back. "You graduated with honors from University of British Columbia," she continued, "then a doctorate from Goiás." Her voice faded into a mumble, then suddenly sounded clear again. "You work fast, don't you? Is that when you met H.F.?"

"No, we'd met earlier, in Vancouver. He's the reason I got into the program at Goiás."

"Then he also found you the postdoc at Port Lowell? And arranged the appointment to SpaceHab?"

"It's all on the record." He shifted again in his seat and felt a flush of anger creep up the side of his neck. He'd had enough of her probing. Pushing aside his untouched coffee, spilling a pool of it into the saucer, he stood before Montague reached the point in his life where Summer entered it. "I'll see you in the morning."

She wheeled away from her data unit and made a move as if to follow him. "Do not worry, Landon. I know patient confidentiality, perhaps better than you think. Trust me on this. Now you must go and let me work. Call H.F. and tell him one more day. This mission goes nowhere until cryogenics is up and running." She chuckled, as if she'd made a joke, and turned back to the mess on her desk.

He exhaled slowly, feeling his knuckles tighten. People kept telling him not to worry, but did he look worried? He wasn't worried, at least not about her work ethic. "I'll see what I can do, doctor."

"I'm sure you will," she said. "And another thing, Landon Alfred Walker. If you insist on using titles, I prefer 'doc.'" She dazzled him with an innocent smile, which looked as out of place on her as it would've been on his father, dying while doing what he loved the most. "By the time we launch, I will know you better than you know yourself."

That, however, was something that *did* worry him.

# Chapter Twelve

VAN PELT'S LAB WAS LOCATED in the easternmost cluster of buildings. By the time Walker found the place, he was drenched and shivering, but not entirely due to the cold rain. Montague was going to delay the mission. The more time they put between themselves and the tachyonic emission, the harder it would be to find it again. His career, his entire reputation hinged on that emission.

Which was why he felt compelled to find Van Pelt. He rehearsed in his mind how he would approach his colleague so that his interference wouldn't appear as such. Colleague, perhaps, but he'd only met the fellow a couple of times at annual symposia. Even though they were both working with tachyons, they really didn't have much in common. Walker's work was far more practical, dealing with communication, while Van Pelt was the theorist. Nonetheless, Van Pelt was a decent enough man who would have at his disposal all the components necessary to collect the Centauri emission. All Van Pelt needed was a little consultation, which Walker would be happy to provide, free of charge. A capture by a second lab would only boost Walker's credibility.

Odd, that this place was so still in the middle of a workday, Walker thought.

Then he remembered that this was a weekend, not a workday for everyone. Still, techs should be here monitoring experiments. Surely the man hadn't given his staff the day off?

Third laboratory on the left, the net directory had told him. From this end of the gloomy hall, he could see gray light spilling from the indicated doorway. Good, the lab was open. Walker stepped softly to muffle the sound of his steps on the glazed floor. Perhaps he would get lucky and slip in without anyone around, assess the situation himself, make a private adjustment or two, then go in search of the tech who was somewhere in the building. Having a coffee, no doubt.

But this wasn't his lucky day. He peered around the doorjamb and saw a young woman, fingers poised above a keyboard as she frowned at a screen.

"Excuse me," Walker said.

The woman jumped. "Shit! Who the hell are you?"

"I have an appointment with Dr. Van Pelt. Have you seen him?"

"His office is the next one down the hall." Her head jabbed in one direction. "But he doesn't like to be disturbed while he's writing journal articles."

"Oh. Perhaps I have the time of my appointment wrong. He asked me to take a look at his equipment. It may not be necessary for me to bother him at all." Walker stepped inside the laboratory, looked around, and waited for an invitation to proceed.

"You'd better check with him first. He's pretty touchy about his equipment, so to speak."

"Yes, well, okay. Next door, you say?"

"That's right. What'd you say your name is?"

Walker ducked back into the hall and hurried along to the office next door. He knocked, then knocked again when there was no answer. Holding his ear next to the panel, he listened for a sound from within, but heard nothing. No typing, no muttering, no coughing, nothing.

Then a chair scraped the floor somewhere in the building, and the young woman he'd encountered in the lab poked her head through the doorway out into the hall. "Hey, you," she shouted.

Walker tried the doorknob, and to his surprise, it turned. He pushed inside before the young woman could stop him.

Inside the office, just behind the desk, a man hung by the neck from a noose strung from the ceiling.

Walker felt as if he'd been punched in the solar plexus. Winded, he staggered against the side of the desk, grasping it for support. On the floor beneath the body was a piece of paper with a single scribble, Tititri. Walker bent down, scooped up the paper, and stuffed it into his pocket before the lab technician barreled inside behind him.

# Chapter Thirteen

ZIZA FONSECA FELT THE MUNDOMBA parasite grow within her. Each day its power grew stronger. She knew this, because she felt its buzz, festering like a nest of maggots. Her mind and her heart warred within her body. Something inside her belly was on fire, whispering at her, urging her to return *home*. To Mãe's jungle. They needed *her*. As she needed *them*.

It was a lie. She'd never in her life wanted to step foot in that fetid place, not for a single moment. Yet, here she was, paddling a boat somewhere up a narrow tributary, she didn't know which one. She didn't know how she'd ended up here, but here she was in some pocket of preserved jungle. The full moon guided her. She'd worked all day for Doctor Inez — she remembered that much — so where she was now must not be too far from the compound in Goiás. Why she was drifting away from the safety of her work, she did not know. Sometimes she felt like an observer inside her own body, and someone else was pulling on her puppet strings, making her do things she knew not what she was doing.

Her arms ached from paddling. The boat bumped against wood and brushed through leaves that clogged the water. Finally, the hull of the boat slid into sticky mud, where it was too shallow to go any farther, even for this flat-bottomed boat. She lurched forward from the jarring stop. Voices floated out from the tangle of trees. Hands tore the paddle from Ziza and pulled her from the boat. Surrounded by women, she stumbled and sloshed through soggy branches. Soon, she tripped up onto a platform, floating atop the water and anchored to a tree.

They were waiting for something. Ziza took this opportunity to look around, drinking in the night in the *igapó* — jungle where floods seep in. Moonlight bathed the scene with silver, making it a ghostly day. The platform loaded with women bumped against a gutted tree trunk. Chirrups and grunts throbbed in the background.

These were the same women who'd helped Ziza bury Mãe. Afterwards, Ziza had slipped away from this dark place of her origins, fleeing in the middle of the night back to Goiás. Back to the scientists.

But now something had made her return here, where nothing ever changed in the *igapó*. Nothing changed except the tributaries that rose and fell with the seasons.

The tea-colored waters still squiggled along a million capillaries deep into ancient forest, and the air felt thick as a wet blanket. The moon sailed overhead like a roving eye, sprinkling its moondust and moonroses in vines that sprouted around tree skeletons, their branches reaching from the swamp to the sky.

One woman who was fatter than sin pressed her back against the tree trunk that supported this platform. A helper carefully placed the garland of fish head skulls around her neck, and another helper pulled a parasitic vine down from the hollow branches of the tree. The fat woman was chosen as the new Mundomba priestess to replace Mãe.

The helpers wrapped the vine around their new priestess, whose rolls of fat began to tremble. Night-blooming flowers awakened and shook off an aroma like no other perfume Ziza had ever experienced. She inhaled deeply savoring its fragrance. She felt a little dizzy, and one of the women standing next to her steadied her.

A flask passed from woman to woman. When it came to Ziza, she wanted to shake her head. No! But something burned inside her, demanding her to drink. She drank.

This was where she belonged.

Along with the other women, Ziza raised her arms to the moon, and together the women summoned the moon spirits to the *igapó*. Blossoming moonrose vines helped the priestess capture the spirits.

"We are...Tititri..." the spirit in the fat priestess told Ziza and her Mundomba women. It was the same voice that had spoken through Mãe. "We come to you...wait for us..."

The parasite inside Ziza stirred, shaking her from the inside out. She couldn't breathe. She felt as if her lungs had flooded, cutting off her air. Panic consumed her with the knowledge of approaching death, and she collapsed in a quivering heap onto the platform.

Ziza didn't die.

In fact, she felt reborn when she awoke some time later to rosy streaks of dawn. Not strangled. The parasite had stolen time from her once again. *Wait for us.*

She wasn't going to die. Had Ziza heard wrong before? Now she had to wait. Not die.

The thought of waiting lingered in her mind. A renewed purpose filled her. She never really had betrayed her Mundomba women. Now, she would have to return to Goiás. Fast, before she lost her job. That's where she would wait for them. And for her parasite's emergence.

# Part Two

Rebecca S.W. Bates

# Chapter Fourteen

*IX MONTHS LATER...*

The night throbbed with samba in the streets of Rio, and Greer couldn't join the world's largest party. Damn! She was excited coming here to Brazil, excited the mission had been delayed, but now? Stupid ISA thought they could keep her locked up. As if she — *Greer* — knew anything worth stealing.

She and Molilia stood on the balcony of the penthouse ISA owned in the residential neighborhood of Leblon and watched the streets below. This was as close as she could come to the swarms of frenzy down there. A sea of revelers, keeping time with the rhythm of samba, displayed bare skin, glistening with sweat, swaying feathers, and bobbing pinpoints of light. Stretching from one mountain to the next, the beach avenue streamed with its crowd surging along like the tide.

Greer had seen this phenomenon before. Aunt Jewel had brought her here once long ago. She'd shown her this unchanging annual ritual of Carnival, as Greer was now showing it to her own niece. "Look, Molilia," she whispered as if she might break the spell. "They're dancing in the streets."

"Biiii," the child responded, pirouetting in her taffeta party dress.

"Yes, honey, 'happy.'" Greer backed slowly into a patio chair and watched her niece stumble, fall, and push herself up onto her feet without a whimper.

Watching the child, she felt her own heart rise and fall with mixed emotions. On the one hand, Molilia had filled an emptiness Greer hadn't even known existed. On the other hand, Greer never had enough time anymore — or adequate funds — to keep up with the constant stream of beauty treatments and social appointments necessary to stay current in this day's world.

And there was Landon, her previously idolized brother. How could he put his work above his daughter?

He was keeping something from her. She'd known it all along. And whatever it was, he was going to end up breaking his neck, or much worse. She had a bad feeling about tomorrow, when the crew members would begin their period of sequester, counting down for scheduled lift-off. She'd at least wormed that much information out of him.

The doors opened behind her, and the sounds of ISA's celebration drifted out into the sultry night, mingling with samba. Laughter bubbled along with the tinkle of champagne glasses.

"Ah, here you are," Landon said, poking his head through the open doorway.

She smiled at her older brother, naive in so many ways. He looked smart, really smart with his trim suit and clean-shaven face. No wrinkles in his collars nor lint on his sleeves for this man. His universe had always been made to order, and that's precisely what annoyed Greer. Landon's order came at the cost of upheaval for everyone else.

Molilia's dancing stopped, and the little girl ran to Greer's side and hugged her knee. Greer placed a soothing arm around the child, the same way Aunt Jewel had done for her. She missed Aunt Jewel dreadfully, and being here for Molilia somehow brought her benefactress back to life for her.

Landon strolled out onto the balcony, thrust his fists into his pockets, and breathed in deeply the thick, salty air. His eyes, as always, were fixed on the ceiling of stars. With that competition, Greer felt invisible.

"I brought Molilia out here to show her the excitement down there," she said, in an attempt to gain visibility. "You'd think all those people in the streets were celebrating this top-secret mission, even though no one is supposed to know about it."

"They know." His gaze lowered from the stars and settled on her. He cocked his head slightly, the way he always looked at her, as if she were a curious item. "Thanks to Inez Pereira and Mario Renato. They've become national heroes."

"Just for being on the mission?"

"It's an honor to be selected," he said in his flat tone of voice.

She couldn't resist teasing him. "If only we could understand why."

"I've already told you — "

"Save it, Landon." She rolled her eyes in what she hoped was a significant gesture toward Molilia, to remind him of the child's presence. "This isn't the time or place to argue about it."

He frowned. She knew that in his mind, any discussion had ended long ago. When her brother had found Van Pelt's body hanging in one of those labs back in the Annex, it had changed him somehow, had made him even more committed to H.F.'s project, if any greater dedication was possible.

Pushing away from the iron railing, he withdrew a small cardboard box from one of his pockets and stepped closer to Greer and Molilia. He knelt before his daughter and presented the gift to her.

Molilia squealed with delight, released Greer's knee, and snatched the box. She waved it in the air, rattling its contents, and pranced around the balcony.

"Go on, open it," Landon said, rising.

Molilia stopped and stared, first at him, then at the box. Her little fingers worked at the lid until she finally removed it. Her face puckered with the threat of a cry as she glanced inside. Landon moved swiftly to her and withdrew a golden chain with a tiny charm, which looked to Greer like a nugget of gold. Molilia waved her arms and stomped her feet, while Landon handed the necklace to Greer.

The golden nugget charm was shaped into a fist, about the size of Greer's thumbnail. Despite its miniature size, she could feel all its details. Ridges delineated fingers. Bent knuckles formed the fist, and the tip of a thumb poked out between the index and middle fingers.

"It's a *figa*," Landon explained.

"Come here, honey, and I'll put it on you," Greer said, fighting back tears. The child would have something to always help her remember her father. Greer had no memento of her father. Nothing, that is, except herself and Landon.

When the child balked, Greer dangled the necklace, holding it out to her. "Come on," she urged.

But Molilia stood her ground and thrust her thumb into her mouth. Frizzy strawberry blonde curls bounced against pale cheeks as she shook her head vigorously.

"Do you feel all right, honey?" Greer dropped the necklace into a pocket and stood. "Landon, is she okay?"

Molilia's color returned as suddenly as it had drained away. She toddled over to a flower and stroked its purple petals with wide-eyed wonder.

"She seems to be okay now," he said.

"What was that all about?" Greer asked, feeling panic rise up in her at the thought of being the sole person responsible for the life of another human being. It was a staggering thought, a staggering responsibility.

He shrugged. "She probably would've preferred a doll."

"The necklace was a very nice thought, Landie. I'll keep it safe for her. Later, when she's a little older, she'll appreciate it more."

He tried to look indifferent, but he didn't fool Greer. "You can tell Molly what Dr. Pereira told me," he said. "Some people think a *figa* brings good luck when it's received as a gift. That's nonsense, of course. But they still make popular trinkets."

"It's more than just a trinket," Greer responded, snuffling. "Excuse me. Watch Molilia for me while I go find the ladies room." Greer sprang for the door before she broke down completely.

Greer slipped inside and closed the glass doors behind her. Leaning against them, she waited for her heartbeat to settle. The climate-controlled air inside calmed her ragged breathing and dried the sticky humidity on her skin. She tried to summon a festive mood to match the occasion. But it wasn't coming. She glanced around the spacious penthouse overlooking Leblon Beach. ISA owned it, in fact the consortium owned the entire building and kept it for entertaining dignitaries when they came to Rio. This showcase apartment reeked of wealth, as it was filled with antique wood and leather. Few people could afford the real thing anymore. Gleaming tables, their surfaces warped from tropical humidity, displayed collectibles from previous centuries, under glass bubbles. Greer thought this furniture was too imposing for comfort.

She glanced over her shoulder and saw Molilia perched on Landon's left hip. He was pointing to something low in the sky out to sea. The finest collection of Brazilian stars sprinkled the area, but she knew which one he meant to show his daughter. Rigil Kentaurus, they called it here, one of the brightest. The child wouldn't understand. Nonetheless, they were absorbed in each other's company.

The restroom excuse forgotten, Greer turned back to the party. In one corner of the room was a pit for viewing holos, and the latest news was showing, attracting a small crowd. She, too, felt drawn to the reports. One man made room for her on the cushions of his bench, sunk down into the pit, inviting her to sit next to him. He had a friendly smile, gray sideburns, and jet-black waves of hair. His waves were the thick, natural kind, not the sculpted kind like Greer's, but even so, he was attractive enough.

He peered at her name badge. "Ah, you're the sister."

She felt a rush of pleasure, being identified. It had been too long since she'd partied. "I guess I am. And you are...?" His badge identified him as Sam Talcott, but that didn't mean anything to her.

"Sam," he said, holding out his hand and grinning broadly.

She shook it. "Do you work for ISA or are you a guest?"

He laughed softly, a pleasant sound. "Both." When she gave him a puzzled look, he explained. "I used to work with the Jupiter team, but now I'm with administration. I don't have a seat on this mission, so I came down here to Rio tonight as Renee's guest." He introduced Greer to the bald woman on his other side.

"Oh!" Greer clapped one hand over her mouth before admitting she'd already met Dr. Montague back in beauty treatment. She couldn't give away her real age, not to a handsome man like Sam, so she swallowed her surprise and changed the subject. "Jupiter? Isn't that where there was some problem a few years back?"

She felt her throat constrict, being reminded that in spite of Landon's confidence, things could always go wrong. Especially when it started out this way, under an umbrella of secrecy. She regarded Sam Talcott with new interest, but before she could pursue her questions, someone turned up the volume on the holo.

"We interrupt this broadcast to bring you a special announcement," said a voice from the holo.

Sam's attention shifted to the woman whose stunningly sculpted body seemed to float out of the screen before them. Greer tensed, recognizing the annoying woman who had broken her promise of payment. It wasn't Greer's fault that Landon hadn't been available. Greer had kept her part of the bargain, after all. She'd tried to arrange the meet-up.

"Good evening, I'm Stephia Drummond with Worlds News Watch," the holo reporter said. "Tonight we bring you a special message from the director of the International Space Agency, Dr. H.F. Washington." Stephia stepped aside, and in her place an old-fashioned desk took shape, popping out of the holo mist. A man with frizzy gray hair sat behind the desk image. He could've been here live in the Rio penthouse, Greer thought, celebrating with the rest of them, but oh no. He had to work instead. Landie's role model.

Deep bags pulled at the lines of H.F's grizzled face, and his eyes were actually bloodshot. It was just like Landon's boss to work so hard that he forgot to take care of himself, Greer thought. Or else he just didn't care. It was no wonder — under his influence — that Landie had grown so serious.

"Good evening," Dr. Washington said. "It brings us great pleasure at the International Space Agency to release the following statement: in this six hundredth anniversary year of Columbus' voyage to the New World, we are preparing mankind's first mission to another star system. Alpha Centauri."

Greer gasped. "That's pretty far! Can they go that far?"

"Shhhh."

Greer bit her tongue as Dr. Washington continued. "On this eve of history in the making, the eight men and women who have been selected to crew a voyage as historic as Columbus', remain in seclusion — "

Laughter erupted from the gathering crowd. Some seclusion, Greer thought as Dr. Washington went on. She recognized six of the hooters: Chico Torres, one of the pilots for the mission, recently out of rehab after some terrible accident. Looked like he hadn't learned a thing from that experience. He was a wiry little guy, full of himself, draped around Inez Pereira, the Brazilian beauty. Mario Renato, the other Brazilian on the mission, squeezed close to Renee Montague, who — Greer knew for a fact — lived up to her image of tough-looking bitch. And Greer recognized Margot Brandt, who was aging badly. Ruy Schulz, an awkward mis-fit, was one of the scientists. They all leaned forward, evidently eager to watch themselves on the holo-cast.

H.F. and his desk dissolved, and Stephia reappeared in all her curvy shapeliness. "Dr. Washington declined an interview beyond the statement you have just heard," Stephia said. "Many of you will be wondering about the suddenness of this mission, and when we asked about that, we were told 'no comment'. But our sources who wish to remain unidentified have told us here at WNW that preparations have actually been underway for at least six months, and — "

Sam made a growling noise. "Who? Who's leaking information to her?"

"We know this for certain," Stephia continued. "Tomorrow begins Phase Two of the project, when a series of launches will begin from the Goiás Launch Site. These launches will use vehicles such as the one you are now seeing on your home screens."

The newscaster's image disappeared again, replaced by a three-dimensional view of an ordinary spaceplane shimmering amidst heat waves that radiated from a blazing red surface. Her resonant voice drifted out of the air. "Each launch from Goiás will deliver two to three crew members, along with supplies, to the Orbiting Launch Pad, where work is underway to transform one of the ships already in ISA's fleet for this daring mission. Sources tell us to expect departure within the next six weeks, although the exact date has not been made public."

The bullet-shaped spaceplane with its desert background flickered and faded. For a few dramatic moments, nothing replaced it, then a gasp arose from the viewers in the room with Greer, as a shiny image surrounded by inky darkness slowly resolved. The object was an oddly connected network of platforms, modules and sails reflecting blinding light as the entire conglomeration hung suspended in black space. The view zoomed in closer, zeroing in on a silvery contraption tethered to one of the platforms. It reminded Greer of three sausage links, but she knew this was a ship because the end link projected exhaust nozzles. The middle link spun slowly, and the forward link sloped gradually to a rounded point where a name was printed in bold, black letters: *ISA Centaurus*.

"What you are seeing now on your home viewers," the announcer said in her clipped tones, punctuated with awe, "is the actual spaceship that will carry its crew of four men and four women to another star. This will be their home for the next twenty-four years. That is to say, twenty-four years will pass here on Earth during their absence, but not aboard ship for them. They will hardly age at all, due partially to the concept of time dilation but mostly to cryogenic suspension. As they decelerate into the Centauri system, the on-board computer will awaken them to perform their various duties. Let's take a look now at who these brave men and women are."

The six crew members in the holo pit with Greer cheered, and the scene shifted from space back to Brazil. On the screen, a group of eight lounged before a hangar of spaceplanes. One of the women, rod-straight and aloof from the others, jumped out from the group in a close-up shot. On the next bench away from Greer, Chico wolf-whistled, and the others chuckled.

"Commander of the Centauri Mission is Joy Masambwa, who comes to this assignment following her daring work retrieving helium-3 from separation plants in the upper reaches of Jupiter's atmosphere. Commander, a word with you, if you please. Are you concerned about the relative hastiness of putting together this mission, as compared to the years of preparation required for previous ventures into space?"

"Not at all," Masambwa answered, her expression unchanging. "Each member of my crew has spent a lifetime preparing for this job."

"What about the setbacks that have plagued this mission? I understand that launch has been delayed twice already?"

Landie's side trip to the Annex, Greer thought, her cheeks flushing. That caused at least one of the delays. He'd had to stay on for questioning about Van Pelt's death. A suicide, they'd finally ruled. Greer bet that Stephia knew all about that fuss, since it had interfered with her plans to interview Landie.

"An unfortunate choice of words," Masambwa said in her monotone. "I would be concerned if we launched before being ready."

"*Is* this mission ready to go?"

"If we weren't, we wouldn't proceed as scheduled."

Greer shivered, wondering if the mission had been rushed beyond the safety factor. No, she decided, they wouldn't push it like that.

"Commander, can you explain to our audience about this matter of time dilation?"

"It's simple enough, due to the ship's enormous speed, relative to your frame of reference on Earth..."

Her explanation was lost on Greer, so instead of listening, she studied the holo image of this single person in whose care eight lives would depend. Masambwa was a shapeless woman, with a military bearing of self-imposed discipline. Impossible to read. Whatever thoughts were going on inside the commander's mind were masked as she droned on.

"A year, you say, of acceleration?" the reporter's voice asked. "And your ultimate cruising speed will approach nearly half the speed of light? Tell me, Commander, how is it possible to achieve such a fantastic speed?"

Masambwa cleared her throat without changing her solemn expression and began, not patiently but still in a monotone. "To put it in layman's terms, our fuel uses deuterium and helium-3, but their detonation is aided by the Fravel Process, which provides the necessary thrust to drive the ship forward..."

"Stupid questions," Sam murmured, nudging Greer. His complaints covered up Masambwa's explanations of the chemical reactions Greer wasn't understanding anyway. "Where do they get these reporters?"

"You mean, what she's saying is...*wrong*?" So maybe it was a good thing she hadn't pulled off Landie's meet-up with Stephia. Greer leaned closer to Sam, hoping that would encourage him to talk. "How so?"

"She always gets it wrong. She's just a pretty face hired by holovision. No brains in residence. Her bosses put her on my ass when I got back last time. She's good at that."

"What about Masambwa? Does *she* know what she's doing?"

He gave her a curious glance, making Greer feel compelled to explain herself. "I mean, you said you worked with the Jupiter team, so I thought maybe you knew her. And since she's apparently not here tonight... I was just wondering. You know."

"Parties aren't her thing," he said with a laugh. "No one really knows Masambwa. She's the only one of us that Jupiter couldn't get to."

"What do you mean?"

"Shhhhh." Sam pointed at the screen where another face now showed in close-up.

Later, Greer promised herself. Later, she'd make a point of getting to know Sam Talcott better and learning all that he knew. She couldn't bear the thought that they were keeping secrets from the public, not when so much was at stake. Including Molilia, who would suffer from an absent, workaholic father. Greer was only thinking of the child.

"Inez Pereira, second in command," the reporter was saying. "Should we call you 'doctor' or 'captain'?"

"Inez will work," she said, laughing.

The six crew members in the room laughed, too, but Sam snorted and shook his head.

Inez, the woman who believed in good luck charms, radiated a sparkling warmth, which reached out across space and time from this staged interview to infect Greer.

Stephia Drummond, the holo reporter, continued. "Would you explain for us, Inez, what your job is on the mission?"

The sparkle clouded over, and Inez looked away. "I will command any extravehicular activity that may be necessary." She took a breath as if to say more, then apparently decided against it.

"Huh," Sam grunted. He whispered in Greer's ear, "Hers and Mario's job is to talk to the aliens."

Greer whipped around to face him. "What aliens?"

He looked genuinely surprised. "Didn't you know? That's what this mission is really about."

"How do you know that?" Her pulse pounded, swishing with a steady beat. Had Landon known about aliens? That would account for all the classified crap he'd tried to feed her. She felt confused. If Stephia Drummond was so stupid, then how come she'd been right, after all? "Are you *sure*?"

"Perhaps I spoke out of turn," Sam said, giving her a lopsided grin. He rolled his eyes back toward the screen.

"We understand that you also serve as astro-linguist, along with Mario Renato," Stephia continued in a more somber tone. "Isn't it true that some*thing* or some*one* is trying to contact us?"

"Damn, there's been a leak for sure somewhere," Sam mumbled.

"What?" Greer asked. Her head hurt.

But Sam ignored her as he concentrated on Inez's response.

"I'm afraid your information is incorrect," Inez said, smiling. "This mission merely serves as another of those 'small steps for man'. We will further our space-faring technology, and we will gather facts. What those facts will turn out to be, it is impossible to guess at this point."

Stephia persisted. "But isn't it true that ISA has received some sort of mysterious message through shaman media around the world? Isn't that why Landon Walker, the so-called expert on a new form of communications, is consulting with the team, training them in the use of his controversial new equipment?

*So-called*? Greer thought, rage steaming through her veins.

"Isn't the real purpose of this mission one of first contact?" the reporter continued. "Isn't that really why ISA is scrambling to get this mission aloft before — "

"No, no, I'm afraid that's complete guesswork." Inez's nostrils flared slightly.

*Before what?* Greer wondered. *Before the aliens come?* And it's the end of the fucking world that Stephia had hinted about.

Inez laughed softly on the holoscreen. "As for Dr. Walker, he is the leading authority on tachyonic communications. He is kindly teaching us how to operate his equipment, which will provide us a vital link to Earth — "

"Good girl," Sam whispered. "That's the story."

"You mean, she's lying?" Greer asked, but Sam was too focused on the holo report to pay her any attention.

Greer thought that Inez's shining face looked as naive as Landon's, and she wondered how such apparent innocence could be a lie. But more than that, if Sam was right, then that meant Landon was lying, too. Not just keeping truths from her, but outright *lying*. Did it have something to do with the haste to launch this mission before...oh god!

But why assume that Sam was right? He was just a stranger to her. Leaning away from him, she wondered what else Sam knew and how he fit into this mission.

Greer twisted around in her cushions to look toward the balcony where Landon, oblivious to the newscast, was still showing Molilia the stars. She'd guessed that he knew more than he was telling her. But was Stephia right and it was *aliens*?

"See here," she said, facing Sam again. Her voice was loud enough to turn neighboring heads. "Where are you getting your information?"

"Shhh," he said, concentrating on the holoscreen.

"But..."

He slipped an arm around her shoulders, a little more firmly than he should've, winked at her, then guided her attention to the reporter. Greer felt like a reprimanded child.

"But not everyone here at home," Stephia was saying, "agrees that we should spend our resources on a mission of this nature, no matter that it's privately funded. Leading this opposition is a terrorist organization that calls itself 'The Savers'. Immediately following this broadcast, WNW will air a special report on the Savers and whether or not they've formed an alliance with grass-roots shamans of the worlds, the very shamans who channel the purported message."

Sam snorted.

"There's a message?" Greer felt her heart skip a beat.

Sam shushed her.

"Our special report," Stephia said, "explores the question of shaman claims about the imminent rise of a new leader, one who supposedly will save us from the doomsday end that the Savers predict — "

Someone, the wizened blonde woman, Brandt, Greer thought, flicked off the holo. "Rubbish."

"That woman won't rest," Sam said, leaning back, "not until she gets her story."

"What story? Is she talking about a cover-up?" Greer glanced around at the six crew members in the room, but they were chatting happily among themselves and not paying Greer and Sam any attention.

A distant look clouded Sam's face as he crossed his arms and examined the ceiling, and Greer thought he'd forgotten her presence, too. Suddenly he said, "Don't believe what she says. None of this goes any farther than this room, you understand?"

No, she didn't understand. Not necessarily. She wasn't the type to believe everything anyone said. But an undefined feeling of panic drummed through her, pulsing in much the same way as the steady beat of samba hammering the air.

# Chapter Fifteen

HUNG OVER THE NEXT MORNING, Greer arrived late to the main building at ISA's Goiás Headquarters. A private sleeper shuttle had brought the partiers back to Goiás from Rio, and after that, Greer spent too much time in her shower in her guest quarters. Soggy as well as late, she stepped off the elevator and balanced Molilia on her hip. She blinked and her head throbbed as she stepped out into a sunny observation room. The glass dome ceiling and sprays of flaming pink bougainvillea, along with other assorted plants, suggested the outdoors, but the air-controlled climate and groupings of overstuffed furniture gave the room a comfortable feel.

"We haven't missed it, have we?" Greer asked, with no one to hear but Molilia. "Where is everyone?"

"Dead," the baby answered, then jammed her fist into her mouth.

"Whaaat?" Greer thought her heart must've stopped. Wide-eyed, she stared face-to-face at the child, squirming to be set down. "What did you say?" Greer demanded again, then realized that of course she'd misunderstood.

It was baby talk. "Dddd," probably. Meaning "Dad." Almost two, and Molilia wasn't talking yet. In fact, her language development wasn't normal. Probably just slow, on account of all those months in cryogenic suspension. Greer couldn't be sure if there was a long-term problem, not without the further DNA analysis Landon wanted. She hadn't seen to that yet, but she would. Maybe she could get that done while here in Brazil. Waiting. Up until now, checking out child centers, trying to get Molilia settled into her new life, and keeping in touch with Landon as much as possible had taken more of Greer's attention than she'd bargained for.

The little girl wriggled down from her hip and toddled away, exploring their new environment. Greer's gaze followed her niece, and she frowned, thinking that she'd miss today's launch for having to watch the child. She sighed from the nuisance and wondered if this was how Aunt Jewel had felt, too, when Greer had first gone to live with her. They were alike, Greer and Aunt Jewel — two settled singles, whose private spaces were invaded by unfamiliar children.

Someone coughed, and a cushion crinkled. Then a head with black, wavy hair peeked around from the side of a tall chair, angled to face one end of the dome.

"Hello," Sam Talcott said, springing to his feet. "You're just in time."

"You!" Greer said, taking a few steps in his direction. "Just the person I wanted to talk to! You slipped out of the party last night before we had a chance to finish our little discussion."

Sam shrugged it off. "Good to see you, too. Come join me for a view of lift-off. We've got the best seats in the house."

She felt torn between watching today's launch — which was why she'd come here in the first place — and grilling Sam about that alien business, but she *should* chase after the baby, whom she could hear jabbering not far away. "I'd better find Molilia before she gets into trouble."

"She's perfectly safe here," said Sam. "You won't want to miss this sight."

Greer hesitated. What did this man know about child care? For that matter, what did *she* know? She was still learning and didn't know what unrecognizable dangers lay hidden in this room. It was full of plants, for one thing. Plants, saved from the Amazon, probably, and who knew what they were? She'd heard news reports that researchers were still finding all sorts of previously unknown compounds from those rescued plants — poisons, and remedies, and god knew what else. But the man worked here, and he must know what was here. Besides, he said it was safe. Letting someone else make the decision for her was a wonderful sense of release.

Sam strode swiftly to Greer's side and took her by the arm. "You can watch her on the monitors from your chair, if that'll make you feel better. Let's hurry. They're about ready to go."

"Where's everyone else?" she asked, as he led her to the arrangement of armchairs.

"It's just us."

"But, there must be more than just *us*. Where are the guests of the mission members? They were at the party last night, so why aren't they here, now?"

Sam laughed, and his eyes twinkled with mischief. "That was a good send-off, wasn't it? A little unorthodox, perhaps, but we decided it was best for everyone's morale. The ground crew enjoyed it, too. They were the 'guests' you saw. Now, sit down." He patted the chair next to his.

"But there're *eight* crew members," Greer said, looking about the empty room.

"It's down to seven now," Sam said. "One of the pilots got bumped."

"Even with seven, there have to be more family and friends than...than, just *us*."

"What kind of people do you think would go on a mission like this?" Sam said patiently. "If they had lives filled with loved ones, do you really think they'd agree to go away for twenty-four years?"

A chill worked its way down Greer's spine as they settled into their chairs. The emptiness of the room reflected a horrible emptiness in each of the lives of the crew. "No," she said in a low voice. "I guess not."

Sam leaned forward to peer through the magnifying lenses inserted in the glass wall of the dome. "It's true that all the crew are loners of one sort or another, but don't look so glum. They've never been happier."

"What makes you think so?" Greer asked.

"Doing something like this is what loners like them thrive on. And when they return, they'll be heroes."

Sighing, she spotted Molilia on her chair monitor and frowned. The child was standing beside a fountain in a rocky arrangement about her size. She held out her arms to the cascading stream of water, then jerked them back, as if in terror.

A good thing to be afraid of, Greer thought, leaning around the edge of her chair to note the location of the waterfall. It recycled into a shallow pool only a few steps away. She could reach Molilia in a matter of seconds, if she had to.

"This is it." Sam's hushed voice pulled her attention back to the view showing the outdoors and the runway where the spaceplane sat.

Activity dwindled around the spaceplane, looking as if launch was imminent. Greer couldn't get out of her head the image of a hive, in whose center the spaceplane glinted under the sun, reminding her of a queen bee surrounded by all of its protectors.

"'Launch' is a misnomer," Sam explained, "a carry-over from the last century. We won't see ignition, not the way the old rockets used to launch. The way these spaceplanes take off isn't much of a show, I'm afraid. All this fanfare is more symbolic than anything."

"Molilia, honey, come see!" Greer shouted.

Beside her, Sam shouted, "what the...?"

———

INSIDE THE SPACEPLANE, a feeling of unease gnawed at Walker as he finished up securing his equipment. The delicate instruments had to be handled properly. The mission couldn't afford any other mistakes.

H.F.'s little party last night had been a big mistake. Walker had tried to warn the old man, but H.F. wouldn't listen. Morale, he'd countered with a knowing chuckle.

Morale could be damned, Walker thought.

Despite the private sleeper shuttle that had brought them home from Rio after the party, the crew had dragged back over-tired to Goiás early this morning. And today they were expected to launch the next phase of the mission on half-drugged brainpower. The first of the supply shuttles would lift off in a few more minutes, starting with this spaceplane. Outside, a flurry of activity littered the tarmac. Only H.F. looked chipper today, scurrying around the various teams out there, but then, he'd had the good sense not to go to Rio to attend his own party.

Walker wouldn't have gone, either, if not for Greer.

The possibility that Van Pelt had also captured the emission preoccupied Walker too much for the distraction of parties. Van Pelt had to have captured it. Otherwise, why else would he have scribbled "Tititri"? But why kill himself over that?

Pushing the questions from his mind, Walker checked off the last of his equipment, making sure the techs had secured everything properly for the transfer up to the Orbiting Launch Pad. Pereira and Brandt were piloting this round of supplies, and now they flicked efficiently through the pre-flight check of instruments, looking and sounding as cool and fresh as if they'd had a full night's sleep.

How did they do it, Walker wondered?

"Last call, Dr. Walker," said Commander Masambwa. She spoke through his earpiece from the control tower.

"Right. I'm going."

A tech hovered by the hatchway, waiting for Walker to clear out so that he could seal the door.

"Don't worry, we'll take good care of your cargo." Pereira looked up from her controls and smiled.

Walker scowled. He wasn't exactly worried, but concerned, yes. He counted each clank and bump of final preparations reverberating through the sleek hull of the spaceplane. He had new pieces of delicate equipment aboard, and if those techs did something to misalign them, the repair would be complicated. Perhaps too difficult for the crew he'd trained. Had he thought to include *every* tool and necessary part that they would need in the next two and a half decades? He'd better have, otherwise, this mission would be pointless.

"Have a good flight," he said, heading for the doorway.

"You're not hitching a ride?" Brandt said.

Very funny.

Walker paused, blinking in the sunlight flowing through the open hatch. Something felt wrong. Not Brandt's lame attempt at humor, either. But he couldn't put his finger on it.

Something sparkled out there against the backdrop of red plains. That's what Walker had noticed, the out-of-place disturbance. A fast-moving vehicle — not surprising in itself — but that it was coming *here* on a dead run toward the spaceplane, could only mean trouble.

All work support was supposed to clear the area, not congest the runway.

H.F. — what was he doing down there? Walker had told the old man to sit tight in his tower, to watch the launch from the comfort of a chair. They didn't need him here. But H.F. hadn't listened. The delays to the mission had worn him down, and coming out here today, directing traffic personally, was his way of taking back control. At least, that was Walker's theory.

H.F. was still down there, waiting for Walker to emerge from the spaceplane, waiting for the tech to seal the hatch, waiting, waiting. From the looks of H.F.'s waving arms, he'd seen the approaching object, too.

One by one, the array of trucks surrounding the spaceplane separated, one vehicle at a time, and headed back toward the white buildings of Headquarters.

They were watching from the tallest one. Molly and Greer. From the observation room, beneath the control tower. Suddenly Walker felt overwhelmed by the magnanimity of this mission, and his small part in it. He felt light-headed — not enough sleep, and too much rush. Too many eyes on him. He swayed on his feet.

H.F. waved at him, trying to get his attention. The approaching vehicle must be bringing an urgent message to them. Abort take-off? Why couldn't they just broadcast their message over the net?

Then it must be a message the control tower couldn't risk anyone overhearing.

Walker's gut cramped.

The last of the trucks had left, except for the one H.F, Walker, and the last tech would use to clear the area. Now the sparkle drew close enough that

Walker could see it was an automated shuttle cart, careening toward them. What urgent message could a driverless cart contain? Perhaps it had been sent to pick up these last three for the brief ride back to the tower. Someone had made a mistake, not realizing that H.F. already had a truck.

It was a mistake, all right.

The cart was moving too fast. It appeared to be on a course that would bypass H.F. As if it headed straight for the spaceplane, instead. Why wasn't it slowing down, Walker wondered? Someone had programmed it wrong, no doubt.

Suddenly H.F. lunged toward the cart, moving with a speed Walker had no idea the old man was capable of. He flung himself onto the cart, tottered and nearly fell off it, then righted himself and tumbled into the control seat. His arms flailed about, wrestling with the controls, and then the cart swerved, tipping so that one edge lifted from the ground.

A cold vise took hold of Walker's heart as he realized — too late — always too late...

"No!" Walker shouted.

The cart rolled off the tarmac, carrying H.F. with it, lurching into the surrounding field, where it exploded into a fiery ball. The boom of the explosion shoved Walker back. Even from the hatch where he stood, frozen, powerless, he could feel the heat of the flames as the cart — and H.F. — exploded into bits and pieces far afield.

"H.F!" Walker screamed and scrambled down the ladder.

# Chapter Sixteen

G REER TORE HER GAZE AWAY from the view of the spaceplane and glanced down at her monitor, at the waterfall view that showed an empty scene. She leapt out of her chair.

"Molilia!" she screamed, running toward the fountain. Shallow, but a pool all the same.

A matter of seconds, that's what she'd said. That's all she'd need to reach the child. Stupid, stupid!

Greer stumbled against the rock wall lining the edge of the pool, the wall where Molilia had sat only seconds ago. Water misted her from the stream that trickled into the shallow water. Face up, under water, green eyes wide open, lay the baby.

———

*FACES. ROWS AND ROWS OF FACES. Side by side, face up, wide-eyed, staring faces. Bodies, corpses really, not people any longer. On account of the water lapping over them, smothering them, flooding their lungs, their wide-open eyes and mouths. You can almost hear their screams. But for the water. The water that stills their cries.*

———

ONLY, IT WASN'T THE BABY'S FACE that rippled under the waterfall. A woman's features had transposed themselves onto Molilia's body, attached like some sort of parasite —

Greer scooped the baby out of the water. This was no dream. Oh god, oh god, what had she done? She'd let her attention wander for a minute, only a minute, and now Molilia was going to die. Probably dead already. What good was Greer as anybody's caretaker?

Sam suddenly materialized at her elbow and grabbed the child from her arms. Brushing Greer aside in the process, he laid Molilia down on the tile floor. Through a blur of tears, Greer watched him work over her niece. Water — or slobber — dribbled from her mouth, then she coughed with a deep, gurgling baby belch.

"Honey!" Greer screamed, pushing her way past Sam.

Molilia blinked from her own child's face again. Yet, the woman under water that Greer had seen, if only for an instant, had seemed so vivid. So *real*.

"It wasn't her face!" Greer screamed. Except for the wavy lines that blurred the woman's features together, it would've been a beautiful face, beautiful in the classical sense of some Greek goddess.

What was she thinking?

Molilia the baby coughed again, and looked around the room, as if she were seeing it for the first time. Then her gaze locked onto the adult faces staring down at her, and her thumb jabbed into her mouth.

Her eyes, Greer thought, were somehow different now. A different shade of green? Yes, that was it. Before, they'd been blue-green, like the northern seas. Greer was positive, but it would've been nice to have Landon's confirmation. Who else knew this child? Who else could tell Greer that she wasn't losing her mind?

Now, Molilia's eyes appeared almost emerald, an unnatural shade for eyes, more like a Caribbean sea, touched with a sparkle of gold.

Greer reached for the child, more to steady herself than to calm Molilia, who seemed perfectly calm. Had there been something in the pool of water that had affected the baby's *eyes*? Oh shit, now what? Greer had never felt so alone.

But she felt even more alone when Molilia pulled back from Greer's touch. "Come here, honey, let me see if you're all right."

"She's all right," Sam said, resting a soothing hand on Greer's shoulder.

"No, no, no, no." Molilia pushed herself onto her feet, backed away from the adults, and promptly landed on her diapered rear end.

Greer followed her and lifted her up, but the toddler stiffened in her arms. She arched her back, flinging her head backwards, and screamed. Greer could take a hint, and she released Molilia, who slid down to a crumpled, sobbing heap on the floor.

Poor little thing, Greer thought. She needed her daddy.

And what about herself? It was more complicated than that, since Greer had already spent most of her life separated from her brother. The hallucination — there could be no other explanation for the woman's face — had to be the result of Greer's agitation for whatever dream her brother was chasing.

# Chapter Seventeen

HE SAW THE EXPLOSION OVER AND OVER in his head. The memory of the erupting ball of flame wouldn't leave him alone. Each flame roiled and then shot outwards from the ball in snapping, hissing tongues of orange to red to black. Again and again.

The days since the accident blurred past Walker as he stumbled from one hastily called meeting to the next. Closing his eyes, opening his eyes, blinking... Nothing shut out the memory of the thundering boom and the geysering shower of flame. For brief moments he could push the fireball to the darkened edge of his mind, only to be replaced by the memory of Van Pelt's body dangling lifelessly from a rope. They'd ruled that one a suicide, and at the time Walker had felt satisfied with the judgment.

But now he didn't know. Someone had murdered H.F. Was it possible that Van Pelt's death had also been murder? If someone had forced him into that noose...and left him hanging there to die... Maybe in the few minutes before death Van Pelt had found a scrap of paper and a pencil in a pocket — those theoreticians usually always carried something to write with. Van Pelt had written "Tititri," perhaps intending to reveal his murderer's identity, but he'd died before he could finish his message.

What mattered was that Van Pelt had captured the emission, too.

Walker sighed. Tititri. The memory of that word had inscribed in his brain, but he couldn't recover any more than recognition. Maybe it was just the mission that was coloring his memory.

The mission would go on, regardless of the monstrous gap that tore through ISA with H.F.'s loss. Even in death, his driving force lived on. All seven remaining crew members were — if anything — all the more dedicated to fulfilling H.F.'s dream. Living his legacy.

The board that H.F. left behind to carry on without him appointed Sam Talcott as acting director, a man who was less qualified for the position than others. Like Walker, for one. But Walker had other problems on his mind right now. He was too busy to take over a desk job, even if it had been offered. Which the board should've done.

Walker had been fast, but not half as fast as the techs who'd arrived on the scene of the fireball, dousing the flames. They gathered up charred remains and threw them all into cryo storage for the miracle of reconstruction that loomed on the horizon of H.F.'s many endeavors. Not that saving H.F. was likely at this point, but who knew what the future held?

Meanwhile, the future was all up to Sam Talcott.

The spaceplane carrying Pereira and Brandt and Walker's equipment had been rattled by the bomb, but not damaged. After an emergency abort, after the debris cleared and systems were checked out, and after Walker re-checked his equipment for the hundredth time, the spaceplane eventually did take off. Now Pereira and Brandt were safely aboard the Orbiting Launch Pad.

In spite of the Savers' attempt to stop them. Yes, Savers. H.F. had said the Savers were done — finished — but he must've been wrong. Who else could've been behind that attack but Savers? It had to be them. Somehow, Savers had infiltrated ISA security. If squatters could, then so could Savers.

But this time, Walker realized, Pereira couldn't have let them inside. Why would she let in her own assassins? Because this time the spaceplane — with Pereira at the controls — had been the intended target. She would've been dead if H.F. hadn't sacrificed himself to save the ship.

The Savers might've slowed H.F.'s dream, but they hadn't killed it. Not long after H.F.'s memorial service, Chico Torres and the geologist Ruy Schulz flew the next shuttle up to join Pereira and Brandt at the OLP. And two weeks from now, the last shuttle would take Mario Renato, Renee Montague and Commander Masambwa. Soon afterwards, with the entire seven-member team re-assembled, the *ISA Centaurus* would launch from the OLP. Walker could imagine H.F. chuckling with the glee of ultimate triumph. And triumph *would* be theirs.

Some triumph, Walker thought with a grunt. It would come at a cost of destroying his family. Molly... Greer... H.F. had been like a father to him, and now he was gone.

Walker wouldn't rest until he'd avenged H.F.

He started with the charred remains of the cart, but whoever had programmed it had been careful to wipe clean any evidence of tampering with programming. The device had blown the dashboard apart.

The last thing he wanted to do was dredge up the memory of his ex-wife, but if Summer's band of terrorists had anything to do with H.F.'s murder, then by god, he'd hunt them down. He'd wrest the information out of her.

He started by reviewing the files of her trial. He flinched to see her looking so dazed. Incoherent. She kept mumbling, repeating the same nonsense. It made no sense. Too much background noise. He edited out the interference, raised the volume of her voice, slowed down her sound, and...

"Tititri." There it was. Walker counted at least five times that Summer uttered the word "Tititri."

Next, he called up Patagonian officials, who reluctantly hauled Summer before their talk screen. She refused to answer Walker's questions. Even across the miles, he could read her sorrow on her face. In the sagging lines that dragged down her once mischievous eyes.

"Tell me who," he raged at her. "You know, don't you? Who from your gang is here in Goiás?"

Silence.

"They tried to kill me." Not just once, he thought, but twice. Maybe the bomb on the cart had been targeted for the spaceplane because *he* was aboard at the time. "They *did* kill H.F. Tell me who did it, dammit!"

She winced as if he'd slapped her.

"You and your friends can't stop the mission," he shouted. "Why are you so intent on trying? Is it the Tititri? Are they behind this? What do you know about Tititri? Is that who killed H.F.?"

She looked up at him. Fear glazed her eyes. "It's started," she said barely above a whisper. "We tried to warn you, but you wouldn't listen."

"How can we listen if you kill us? What have you got to say that'll help?"

"Prepare."

"Prepare? For what? Aliens? You think they're coming to get us?"

"Don't let them take her."

Summer's non sequitur only enraged him further. "Take who? So you and your gang of thugs want to kill us all in order to keep the aliens from killing us? Is that what you think? Look. If you tell me who's behind this, then it doesn't have to be too late. Maybe we can do something. Tell me, dammit, and I'll do everything I can to get you transferred out of there. Somewhere better. All you have to do is tell me who it was." She knew, dammit. He knew that she knew.

But in response, Summer hummed a discordant melody, as if flaunting her craziness in his face. "Teee-teee-treee," she sang, her voice growing louder with her defiance.

Goosebumps tickled Walker. *We are Tititri.* He tried again. "Who, dammit?"

"Mollll-eeee. Don't let them take Molilia."

Walker sighed. Now she was throwing Molly in his face, reminding him of how she'd controlled that situation from the get-go. He slammed down on disconnect. It was no use getting through Summer's warped mind. Talking sensibly to her was impossible. Seeing her again, trying to talk, only stirred up all the bitter memories. She probably didn't even remember him, that's how warped her mind was these days.

But where had she come up with Tititri?

———

WALKER WENT FOR A RUN to let off the steam that the effort of talking to Summer had left with him. He followed one of the cleared trails through a debris-strewn field of dried mud between the main building of headquarters and the landing strips. A couple of miles later, he paused to sit on a rock and brood.

Molly was safe with Greer, and both of them were safe in the visitor's quarters of this compound. Safe? Sure. He had to believe that, despite the security breaches, otherwise he'd go nuts.

Of course no one would take Molly away. What had Summer meant? Probably the old fear that Summer had been taken away from Molly. Well, she'd chosen her path when she signed on with the Savers.

The Savers...the Tititri... Were they connected somehow? Was that what Summer's demented mind meant?

In the distance, he noticed a small dust cloud rising. Someone followed him along the trail. He watched the object causing the dust as it drew nearer, and finally he could make out its mechanical shape — a cart. Like the one that had killed H.F.

Dread washed through him. He jumped up from his rock and ran on, but all the while he knew he couldn't outrun a cart, not if it had been programmed to intercept him on this trail. He turned off the trail. And so did the cart.

He ran faster, sprinting over the loose rubble. But he couldn't always direct where his feet landed, and when they landed wrong, they slid beneath him, costing him precious time as he fought his balance. Slowly, he gained on headquarters, but so was the cart gaining on him. Still, he ran on.

The cart didn't blow. If it had been loaded with a time-triggered device, then when was it set to go? He couldn't outrun it, but he'd bought some time. Maybe it was triggered for his DNA. Or for impact. The main building lay dead ahead. He couldn't risk an impact there. Better to die out here, alone. He stopped and waited for the cart to catch up. When it did, it stopped beside him, as if waiting for him to board. A woman's melodic voice called to him from the cart's speaker.

"Message for Dr. Walker," the cart said.

He muttered under his breath and stepped on. No bomb.

The cart wheeled around, taking him away from headquarters, over to one of the neighboring laboratories. Along the way, Walker watched its dashboard, trying to determine its programming. Lights blinked and numbers flashed.

The cart rolled into a storage bay and shut down. Okay. He stepped gingerly down from the running board. Nothing happened.

Someone wanted him here. That's all.

He swiped his hand across the sweat streaking his face. So where was whoever'd summoned him? He walked to the doorway and peered into the next laboratory.

Colored lights blinked from the walls, and a young woman stood there, watching the lights as her fingers moved swiftly across a hand-held device. She looked up as he entered.

"Dr. Walker?" she said. "There's a delivery here for you. I sent the cart out for you. Was your remote turned off?"

"So it was *you* who sent that blasted thing after me, then?"

The woman's eyes rounded to white saucers. She gulped air as she explained. "He said it was urgent. He said you'd want to see it right away. He told me to find you."

"Who said?"

She consulted her hand-held. "Jackson?"

Walker's assistant from SpaceHab. "Where is it?"

"Right over there, in the inbox."

"And who are you?"

"My name is Ziza Fonseca."

He found the data stick labeled for him and plugged it into the mail reader. It contained readings on the latest emission, collected from his equipment at SpaceHab and transferred here. Great. Now any Savers monitoring them would have access, too. What they didn't have was Pereira's interpretation of the data.

"I need to contact the Orbiting Launch Pad immediately," Walker told the woman on duty here, Ziza something.

"You can do that from Doctor Sam's office," she said, pointing at a door opposite her blinking equipment.

"Sam Talcott?"

"He is the one. Is there another Sam?"

Walker shrugged. "I just didn't know that Sam had an office here."

"Well, he's moved over to the main building since — " But Ziza had the good grace not to mention H.F.'s accident that had prematurely elevated Talcott's position within ISA. "But he still works here sometimes, too."

"Handy," Walker said, glancing over his shoulder at the automated cart holding area.

No. Talcott wouldn't have had anything to do with ordering the cart that killed H.F. It didn't make sense that Talcott would risk jeopardizing the mission for which he'd been hired to ensure its success.

Still... How badly had Talcott wanted the director's chair?

Walker stormed across the lab and yanked open the door to Talcott's office. He sat down at the desk and sent a call through to the OLP. He could hardly wait to hear Pereira's so-called translation of this latest emission.

# Chapter Eighteen

ZIZA FONSECA DIDN'T WANT TO DIE. She'd do anything for Doctor Inez, but dying wasn't one of them.

The most that she would agree to do was work for the new boss Doctor Inez had found for her. Ziza didn't want to work for anyone else, but she didn't blame her boss, who was being sent away to some distant place. Why not send Ziza away, too?

Ziza's new job was simply to watch a wall of blinking lights. When they blinked correctly, it meant that the machines were working. What these machines did exactly, she didn't know, but it had to do with the project of recording obscure languages before they disappeared forever. Sometimes she watched her fingers turn dials and knobs, almost as if her fingers had a life of their own. She didn't know. The lights blinked in tandem with the humming buzzing squiggling parasite inside her, and she felt a glow of peace.

Safe. The parasite was finally safe, as its people would be soon. All Ziza had to do was wait.

Sam Talcott breezed into the lab, shouting for her. "Ziza?"

She couldn't see her new boss, but she could feel the power of his rose quartz talisman drawing her to his will. She cringed from the edge to his voice, which reminded her of machetes slicing through moonflower vines.

"What the devil are you doing out there in the cart bay?" he said. Or was it the rose quartz speaking to her through the parasite? Sometimes the voices that filled her head confused her.

She gulped in the charged air, and it startled her, as if awakening her from Mundomba trance. For the first time she saw rows of carts surrounding her. Her fingers flew across the hand-held device she carried. What *was* she doing here?

"Just checking security, sir."

"Ziza, you are so efficient. But just because the cart bay is next door to our lab doesn't mean that securing carts is part of your job. You don't have to worry about the saboteur who broke in and tampered with one of them. It's not your job."

Ziza knew her job, and she wasn't worried. It was too bad about Dr. Washington, but —

"Not to worry," Doctor Sam went on. "What I want to know now is about the new message we've received. Did you send Walker to my office to open it?"

"Where else?"

"Good!"

He spoke with too much enthusiasm, she thought. Doing her job — whether or not she remembered doing it — was nothing out of the ordinary. "Do you feel all right, Doctor Sam?" His pale skin flushed, and he breathed hard, as if he'd run the entire distance here. What was so important, she wondered, about that message Doctor Walker received?

"Never better, Ziza. I owe Dr. Montague for the spectacular state of my health. And your drugs, of course."

Her heart beat rapidly with alarm. Or perhaps it was the parasite that drummed her heart faster. "I have no drugs."

He laughed. "Figuratively, that's what I mean. The drugs Dr. Montague used on me after my Jupiter mission came from the rainforest. Your home. Who knew what wonders are still locked up there?"

"My home is here, Doctor Sam." The parasite came from there. It pulled at her, tying her back to that place of her origins. She dreaded the wait, and at the same time, she couldn't wait for it to leave her alone. But still, she didn't want to die. Once the waiting was done.

"Ziza, do you like working here?" he asked. The change in his voice made her look up at him.

"Doctor Inez sent me here," she said.

"And she was right to bring you to me. But Ziza, you don't have to think of your job for her as over. You are still working for her."

"I work here now, and she is gone."

"That's right. But what you do for me is really for her. Do you understand?"

"No."

"Well, never mind about that just now. Let's see what you've got." He turned away and marched out of the cart bay, back to Ziza's blinking machine.

She trembled with fear. The parasite had told her that the spaceplane had to be stopped. She was sorry that Dr. Washington had died — he'd gotten in the way — but she was even sorrier that she had failed. The spaceplane hadn't been stopped, and now the carts wouldn't obey her commands anymore. What would her people do to her?

"This is what Inez sent?" Doctor Sam yelled at her.

"It just arrived. You want I send cart for Doctor Walker again?"

"No, no..." Doctor Sam moved closer to the screen. "It's not just another audio message. There's something visual here, too. It's a damn lot of pixels, isn't it?"

# Chapter Nineteen

**T**HEY PICKED AT EACH OTHER like schoolboys, all throughout dinner. Greer was so embarrassed. What on earth had gotten into Landie? He was acting the part of the over-bearing big brother, grilling her new beau, who in this case was Sam Talcott.

She wished.

"Why don't you get to go on the *Centaurus* with them?" she asked Sam over crab appetizers. Sam had organized this send-off party, a small affair in the atrium observation room, and Greer only meant to make polite conversation.

"Can't. Medical disability."

Her gaze swept across his fit body, posture-perfect at the head of the table. "You look like you're in perfectly good health to me."

He laughed. "Thank you, ma'am."

That had started Landie's tirade. "Looks have nothing to do with it, Greer. When are you going to learn that?"

"Leave her alone," Dr. Montague said. A crumb of pastry clung to the edge of her mouth. "Good health is what matters, and Sam is well on his way."

"On his way where?" Landon said. Greer didn't like the sound of challenge in his voice. She tried again with Sam.

"So, what do you do now? I mean..." She blushed and stammered. "Why did Dr. Washington want you here, even if you can't go along on the voyage?"

"At first, I was supposed to help expedite the training, since they needed to get this mission off the ground so fast."

Landon snorted.

"Well, I think you throw a nice party," Greer said with a giggle.

She'd felt like a prisoner, waiting in Goiás with Molilia in the apartment ISA provided. The days dragged by while Landon helped the Centauri crew go about their final preparations to leave Earth. What did these people in Goiás do for amusement? Sam tried his best to suggest entertainment, and Landon tried his best to boss her with unreasonably cranky orders not to see Sam.

Up until tonight, group meals always took place in a cafeteria in one of the laboratory buildings, where chemical smells permeated everything, including the table linens. Greer regaled whoever was present with the tale of Molilia's "little adventure" under the waterfall and the face Greer thought she'd seen. It was a hallucination, she explained, caused by her own panic, and her dinner companions politely asked to hear more. Greer was a social success, but the only company she ever really wanted was Sam's. Especially now that he was supposedly off-limits to her, according to Landon the dictator.

Then, late this afternoon, with only two more days to go before the last launch up to the orbiting *Centaurus*, Sam appeared at the front door of Greer's apartment with a local woman named Ziza Fonseca. She was a golden-skinned woman with a face as round as a melon and a smile as warm as a Caribbean vacation. ISA had done a full background check on the woman's history, Sam informed Greer, and Ziza was to care for Molilia while Greer and Landon attended the little send-off party he'd organized for tonight. It was a small affair, nothing as elaborate as what H.F. had done down in Rio. Still, Landon grumbled.

Greer spent hours choosing her wardrobe. She was getting a night out, away from the baby for a change, and she felt released. She felt almost drugged with excitement, like a young girl again. Wait, she was still twenty-nine, wasn't she?

And when she stepped off the elevator with Landon into the observation room, she squealed with delight. Lights sprinkled through the foliage of the atrium, enchanting her with its magical, festive feel. No matter how much Landon tried to spoil her mood, she refused to let him.

"Why did you have to get the mission off the ground so fast?" Greer asked over squash soup. The question came to her automatically, as it had been on her mind ever since Landon first visited in the Holland Annex.

"Having been part of the Jupiter team, I'm familiar with the — "

"No, I mean, why do they need to get this mission off so fast? Why can't they take more time to get ready?"

"You mustn't worry," Sam said. "Everything's checked out, and the ship is in top shape. They'll be fine."

He seemed to think that she worried a lot. In truth, it was Landon who worried. "You haven't answered my question," she said, fluttering her eyelids just a bit.

Sam chuckled. "You're not the only one with unanswered questions."

"He refers to all the trouble my department has created." Mario Renato, the Brazilian linguist national hero, laughed.

"Oh?" Greer said. Mario was kind of cute, but he was too old for her. Still, he was definitely interested in her, which flattered her to no end. She led him on. "What trouble is that?"

"Nothing," Landon snapped.

"If H.F. were here," Sam said, "he would disagree with you."

"Only because you coached him in what to think," Landon said.

Sam shrugged. "Perhaps I was instrumental in helping him understand reality."

"And what reality was that?" Greer felt her pulse beat stronger.

"I believe he's referring to his own personal spiritual reality," Mario said.

Greer was confused, and she was only on her second glass of wine. Not counting the champagne that kicked off tonight's party. "Wait a minute. I thought you were talking about some trouble you had? Have you fixed it? I mean, you guys are leaving day after tomorrow on this mission."

"Not Landon nor I," Sam said. "We're staying here."

"The two of you will have the most important job of all, directing us," said Dr. Montague. "The rest of us won't have anything to do for quite a while. The ship will do it for us."

"You'd better not sleep on the job, like us," said Mario with another laugh.

"Then, you're saying there's still a problem?" Greer said. And it was up to Landon to fix it. That's why they wanted him here. Heaven help them. The image of her brother as a problem-solver bubbled in her mind, along with champagne, and she hiccupped. Landon gave her a sour look.

"Not exactly," Mario said. "The problem won't really begin until after we get there and Inez and I have to start interpreting. They're hoping that between the two of us..."

The table fell silent as Mario's voice drifted off.

"Wh-who are you going to talk to?" Greer's voice cracked.

"I believe it started in Jupiter, didn't it?" Mario said.

"Jupiter?" Greer said. "What does Jupiter have to do with this mission you're going on?"

"Isn't that where you first met them?" Mario said softly.

"Met who?" Greer spilled her wine.

"No one," Landon snapped.

"He is right," Dr. Montague said, jumping in to the heat of the moment. "It was no one. It was, instead, shall we say...a spiritual encounter."

"Encounter?"

"Experience. Yes, that is what I mean to say. I should know, since I have treated Sam ever since that time."

"What experience?" Greer asked during the meat course. Some local meat. She didn't want to know any more than that. Her head hurt, and she massaged her forehead. No one answered her, and so she went on. "Oh, I get it. It was a spiritual revelation that made you quit being an astronaut and turn instead to administration, right?"

"Greer," Landon said, shaking his head and shushing her with the stormy look that crossed his face.

"Well, what? Why won't you tell me?"

"It is similar to the Mundomba belief system," Mario said. "The devout believe that spirits who wish to guide us through life reside in another plain of existence and only speak to us through their representatives here on Earth. The spirits speak through them, advising the people and such."

"Huh?" Greer drank more wine, but it didn't help her follow the conversation.

"In reality, it's not so different from Christianity," Sam said. "That's the reality we're talking about. That's all."

Greer turned back and forth, watching them say words that held no meaning. Her head spun. "Why on earth are you talking religion all of a sudden? Is this mission supposed to find God, or something?"

Sam laughed a light-hearted, reassuring sound, using his not-to-worry tone of voice. "That would be an added benefit, don't you think?"

Landon threw his napkin down onto the table. "That's enough, Talcott."

"What's enough?" Greer said. She was going to get whiplash at this rate.

Sam's eyes twinkled. "Ever since the Europeans first arrived in this hemisphere, they have wished to assert Catholicism over the myriad of indigenous religions. Eventually they sealed the deal in Brazil by erecting the monument known as the *Cristo Redentor*."

"It's ironic, don't you think?" Mario said. "The way the religions assimilated."

But no one answered him. Sam and Landon glared at each other with enough distaste to prevent anyone from uttering a sound.

It was up to Greer to break the silence. "What's for dessert?"

————

ZIZA COULDN'T GET THE VOICES OUT of her head. First, her belly rumbled, and now her head sang to her. First, she thought it was the parasite, but now she understood that it was Mundomba. *She* was Mundomba, and she could not ignore who she was. They called to her, and she knew what she had to do. It wasn't exactly like disobeying Doctor Sam.

Because she couldn't ignore the voices. Above all the rest, it was the voice of Doctor Inez that she heard in her head. And Ziza would do anything for Doctor Inez.

"Now is the time," the voice whispered to her. "She is the one."

# Chapter Twenty

GREER OPENED THE DOOR the next morning to Sam and Ziza Fonseca. He'd made all the arrangements, he told her, for their day's outing to Corcovado. He even claimed that Landon had approved, although that wasn't likely. No one bothered to consult Greer.

She should've declined, as a lesson to his high-handed manner, but she couldn't resist this opportunity. It was too easy, even if an annoying cloud of mystery *did* envelop the former astronaut. How could a man like that, a man whose word she couldn't trust, make her eager to go with *him*, to abandon Molilia in Ziza's care, if just for the day? It must be the boredom, she reasoned. Or perhaps it was his thick waves of black hair, silvering at the temples.

Whatever it was, a tingle of anticipation coursed through her as he drove her to one of the hangars. This all felt so *illicit*. Illicit was always good.

The jetcar was a two-seater, and she strapped in beside him in the pilot's seat. They skimmed over the laser fence surrounding the Goiás compound, separating it from the new tenements of the Amazonas relocation program. A sea of shanties sprawled to the vast horizon. Sitting next to Sam, she had a close look, closer than she'd wanted, of the uneven rows of homes thrown together with cast-off pieces of plastic. Rutted red roads divided them into parcels and harbored piles of garbage and streams of aimless people. Where had they all come from? Hordes of lost souls swarmed around the ISA pe-rimeters, as if looking for a way through the laser beams where they would have room to breathe. Seeing their cramped quarters made Greer feel guilty. Spoiled. Escaping from the compound wasn't producing the exhilaration she'd expected.

So much for the possibility of a romantic interlude, she thought.

They soared over needles and spires of cities passing below, hills, and more plateaus. All the while, Sam told her of his mission to set separation plants in the upper reaches of Jupiter's atmosphere. The Brazilian landscape shifted beneath them to a cloud-shrouded mountain range as Sam explained about those jovian separation plants, where helium-3 was collected from the plentiful atmosphere, to be used as starship fuel.

Finally, the clouds ended, and the land fell away into the famous vista of Rio's mountain-studded bays. The sight took Greer's breath away. Sam's smooth voice captivated her with some story of Masambwa's bravery. Some-thing about manually repairing one of the separation plants that had been damaged by a lightning strike. It didn't matter what he told her. It was his voice that she hung onto, spellbound.

———

IT WAS HIS VOICE THAT GREER HUNG ONTO, spellbound. Or was it the view? In any case, she felt light-headed. Before she could regain her composure, Sam angled the jetcar toward one of the mountain studs, stand-ing bare and rocky. Atop it, she could see the distant outline of a cross.

Sam snapped out of his storybook voice and spoke crisply into his head-set. "Corcovado Patrol, come in, please. This is ISA 881, requesting en-trance."

Static crackled, then a thick accent answered. "ISA, you are cleared to enter."

He turned to Greer. "They already know who we are."

She was sure "they," whoever "they" were, would know far more than she knew. She had a feeling that today's outing was less for her and more of a job that Sam was scheduled to do. "See here, Mr. Talcott, what's this place all about?"

Sam relaxed in his seat and guided the craft around to the back side of the mountain. Below them, a laser fence surrounded the base of the mountain. Within the fenced area, crumbling remains of trees lay like a bed of maggots across the folds of the mountain's terrain.

"Corcovado has been closed to the public for years," he said, "because tourists have destroyed the mountain. Finally, International Parklands seized it from Brazil. They're attempting to restore it, but as you can see, it's not easy."

"If it's closed, then why are we *here*?"

The jetcar lifted itself like an elevator, following the contours of the terrain toward the crown of the mountain. Suddenly, a giant head, encased in a brace of scaffolding, reared up from the top of the mountain. Turned away from them, it gave Greer the sensation of sneaking up on a shackled prisoner. Next, extended arms appeared, along with a slim back.

"But...there's no cross at all," she said with a gasp of wonder.

"Your first time to see the statue up close?" he asked.

Nodding, she opened her mouth, but words evaporated on her tongue. She couldn't tell him that yes, from afar she'd seen the famous statue atop its mountain when Aunt Jewel had brought her to Rio long ago. But her aunt hadn't taken her up Corcovado Mountain then, and as a child, Greer had confused the image. She'd always thought there was a cross somewhere, but now she could see that that had been an illusion. Instead, the entire body of the statue of Jesus was shaped like a cross with arms outspread.

Even through the scaffolding, which completely enveloped the statue, she could feel its melancholic strength radiating through the network of braces and platforms. She was only vaguely aware of the jetcar's floating descent to the tiny strip next to an abandoned tram's terminal.

The silence hit her first as she stepped from the jetcar. Where were all the workers? Jesus embraced the bays of Rio, and she felt like a microbe in his presence. *Its* presence, she reminded herself. It was just a statue. No need to feel reverence. All the same, a shiver worked its way down Greer's spine.

Growing up without a mother, she'd never even been inside a church while her father was still alive. But when she went to live with Aunt Jewel, her benefactress had insisted Greer attend one of them with her. It was a curious ritual, primarily for women. Female bonding, or some such nonsense, Aunt Jewel had called it. Luddism is what Greer called it. But she was grateful for her new home, so she went quietly with her aunt. This fact was a confession she never wished to share with her school chums. Still, she remembered the pleasant way sunshine had fallen through the colored pieces of glass windows and the way those patterns had enchanted her.

She felt enchanted now as sunshine slanted through the clouds hugging the inland mountain range and spotlighted the string of bays laid out before them. Jesus stood over her like her protector. Certainly, something was watching out for them. After all, something had saved Molilia from drowning.

"Breathe," Sam said at her elbow, startling her.

"Sam!" she cried. "It's...it's impressive."

"Wait'll it's restored. The statue will be easy, but the mountain is giving them a hell of a time."

"No, it's the view," she insisted, swallowing hard.

A breeze tickled the designs in her scalp. She held out her arms, statue-like, and felt free, the way a bird must feel floating on the currents of air. However, there were no birds. She was the only one, and she imagined soaring off this perch and floating down, far below, to the city, which remained busy as ever, oblivious to the consequences of its invasion of the land.

"Come with me." He caught one of her hands and led her up an incline, littered with broken chunks of concrete where steps must've been at one time. "Careful," he instructed, pointing out exposed holes in the stone base surrounding the statue's skirts. He paused beside a ladder at the base of the scaffolding.

It made her dizzy to look straight up, seeing the statue in its body brace against a background of blue. High above them, she saw a bird, as if summoned by her thoughts. It floated on an air current, apparently reluctant to get too close to the land. To man.

He nodded. "Shall we?"

She sucked in her breath. "Can we? I mean, where is everyone?"

But Sam only chuckled and hoisted himself up the ladder to the first platform. "Come on."

She followed him up, but by the time she reached the first platform, he was on the ladder again, pulling himself up to the next level. She paused a minute to stare at the feet of this statue, standing regally atop a base of crumbling concrete blocks. Even with toes missing, the statue radiated a power that left her feeling as breathless as the view had made her feel. She must be climbing too rapidly. "Wait," she called, but Sam laughed and kept going. Looking up made her dizzy, so she lowered her gaze to the chipped folds of Jesus' skirt as she continued to climb. Just below the draping sleeve of one extended arm, the platform circled around to the front of the statue.

"Come on, you're almost there," he called down to her.

A wave of dizziness hit her again, but she pushed it from her mind and ascended the last stretch of ladder, up the side of the chest. She could see Sam peering down at her from his perch. By the time she reached him, she was breathing heavily. He held out his hand to help haul her up to his level, and she gasped as she straightened up. Standing, she faced Jesus' chin.

She felt Sam's gaze on her while she stared, transfixed, at the curve of the jaw, which contrasted to the straight lines of hair falling down to the shoulders. The chin protruded, as if with determination, and above it were the lips, sealed together in silent trust and acceptance. She had to crane her neck to look up at the rest of the head, towering above her, showing the chipped ridges outlining a nose and eyebrows. Shadows hid the eye sockets, obscuring his thoughts from her.

*His thoughts?* It was just a statue of a questionably historical figure, she reminded herself, swaying.

Sam caught her by the elbow. "Watch your step," he warned. "It's a long way down."

Only then did she turn to look at him, but still, she couldn't speak.

"Impressed?" he asked with a chuckle.

No, she wanted to say. Religious symbols didn't impress her. But she found herself nodding. Her helplessness annoyed her, but there was something unidentifiably powerful about this statue, and it held her, captive, the same way Sam clutched her. His arm slipped around her waist, and he pressed her against his side. She became aware of the pounding of her heart. Or was it his?

"Are you all right?" he asked.

Again, she nodded. This time she added a difficult swallow. Somehow, she thought she wasn't really all right. She felt slightly nauseous, as if she'd eaten bad food. Her throat felt cracked and dry, yet her palms were clammy with sweat.

"Why should something like this amaze us so much?" Sam asked.

"It's not the statue," she whispered, even though no one was going to overhear. "It's being this close to it that takes your breath away."

Standing at the statue's chin level, she reached out with her hand. Sam's arm slid off her waist as she pulled away, stretching forward, reaching through the grid of the scaffolding, to touch the cool, yes cool despite thick humidity, the cool surface of the stone chin.

"Careful," he warned again, steadying her by planting both hands on her waist, as one might do for a child leaning too far over a railing.

The sound of Sam's voice broke whatever spell the statue had placed over her, and she fell back against his chest, solid and comforting. She turned around to look at him and wondered if maybe, just maybe it was *Sam* who was putting the spell on her. The lines creasing his face indicated the sternness of command, the harshness of a man accustomed to having his way. However, the warmth of his brown eyes, twinkling like a golden autumn, showed his playful nature. This was a two-sided man, Greer decided, and she felt both drawn to his warmth and repelled by his resolute attitude. Shaking her head in confusion, she tried to take a step backwards, away from him, but he held onto her waist in a tight grip.

Then his brow wrinkled. "You're not going to faint on me, are you?" he asked. "You're not afraid of heights, are you?"

"N-no." She shook her head vigorously. "I'm all right. Really." Desire blossomed within her from the firm feel of his touch, and she wobbled against him, tilting her lips up to brush against his face. For a moment, she felt him succumb, and she knew that this time *she* would be the one to have her way.

Then he tensed and pushed her aside. "Later," he said, reaching into his side pocket and withdrawing a hand-held unit. "We have a job to do first."

"The hell?" She crossed her arms and stuck out her lower lip. *He'd* led her on. It wasn't her. She was just letting him know she was available. "Then you can take me home this minute."

He ignored her and flicked open his little device with his thumb. With his other hand, he punched in instructions.

Greer wasn't accustomed to mixed signals. How could she have interpreted his behavior so wrong?

He stared transfixed at his device while a picture materialized on the flipped-up screen. Pursing his lips, he studied the picture, then glanced up at the statue's face. Then back down to the tiny unit he held in one palm.

"What the hell is going on here?" Greer asked.

Rather than answering her, he thrust the device in her hands. "What do you think?" he asked.

She gazed at the picture on the screen. It was a face. Nothing more than a face. It had no gender, no details, no attached body. No life. It was merely a blank face, like the beginning of what an artist might sketch. "So what?" she asked, passing it back to Sam.

He looked up at the statue again.

"Wait. You think it's *him*?" She grabbed the hand-held device from Sam and studied again the crude face it contained. There was shoulder-length, straight hair, the same way Jesus had worn his hair. The chin in Sam's picture was extra long, perhaps because it protruded. Or maybe it was a beard, like what Jesus had. The mouth was a slit, the same slit a mouth would make with closed lips.

"It can't be," he said.

"Okay, so it's not."

"You really think it's not?"

He sounded hopeful, but who cared? Why did it matter that someone had done a computerized sketch of Jesus? Sam was just being melodramatic, and it annoyed her that he couldn't be more straightforward. "So why the mystery? Where'd you get this?" She felt her annoyance creep into the sharp edges of her voice.

He looked over both shoulders, as if someone might be spying on them up here. Satisfied that they were alone, he said in a low voice, "This was interposed with the signal they're sending us."

"What are you talking about? What signal? Who?" Greer still felt light-headed from her whirly-gig emotions, and she grasped one of the support beams to steady herself.

"Remember the reporter? Stephia Drummond?"

How could she not remember that woman who'd invaded her home in the Annex? Promised her money and then broke her promise, when it wasn't Greer's fault.

"The holo reporter," Sam said when she remained silent, pouting. "Remember? In Rio, the night of the big send-off." He paused, then when she still didn't respond, he continued, "The party in the penthouse — "

"Of course I remember," she snapped. "I just don't understand what you're talking about."

He sighed and tried again. "On the holo, Stephia asked Inez if we're receiving a message from the Centauri system, and Inez denied it, because that's what ISA instructed her to do."

"You said Stephia was wrong. She always gets things wrong. That's what you said."

He wagged his head and gave her a weak smile. "Sometimes she stumbles onto pieces of the truth."

Greer's knees felt weak, and she squeezed the support beam until her knuckles ached. "Then...it's true?" she managed to whisper. "She said something about aliens invading, didn't she?" Stephia *had* implied that, even if she hadn't actually said it in so many words. That's what she'd meant. "So it's true?" Greer had known it all along, really, but she'd managed to suppress her knowledge with Landon's string of denials.

Sam waved the hand-held at her and nodded. "SpaceHab picked this up a couple days ago. This arrived in one brief burst of light particles, then it was gone. Hasn't repeated since."

"But you've received other messages from aliens before this? Then, that's what Mario was talking about last night. He and Inez have to interpret for aliens, don't they?"

Sam said nothing, and his lack of a denial only confirmed Greer's hunch.

"I knew it," she said. "Why couldn't Landon tell me?"

"We didn't want to start a general panic — "

"I don't panic. He could've told me."

"We don't know what we're dealing with. There's a tendency to panic, before people have enough information to know if panic is warranted or not."

"Why are you telling me about it now? Why'd you bring me here?"

He cleared his throat, and a hint of a flush colored his cheeks. "Some folks think this likeness is from ourselves in the future, but I don't. I think it's one of them. And I was wondering if this was the face you thought you saw. When Molilia was under water."

Shuddering, she made herself remember the ripply features she'd glimpsed against the baby's face. She looked again at the picture in his palm and felt another wave of weakness overpower her. "No. That was a woman. This is a man."

He swore under his breath. "Are you sure? You're being influenced because you know this statue is supposed to represent a man. Look again at the face. By itself, it holds no gender."

She shook her head. It was Sam who was trying to influence her, she thought. Not the statue. "What about the beard? Anyhow, I know what I saw."

"Do you remember that face well enough to be able to describe to an artist who could sketch it for us?"

"Of course I do. But why, Sam? Do you think that woman in Molilia is connected somehow to *him*?" Greer nodded at the genderless face on the tiny screen.

"We don't know. I just thought I should bring you here and let you have a look at the real thing as well as this one." Lost in his thoughts, Sam tapped the screen of the hand-held.

"So...what are you saying? Jesus is...an alien?" She couldn't make her voice function above a croak.

Sam's own face was a picture of concern as he took a step closer to her and encircled her waist with his arm. "Damn. I was so certain. Somehow... Molilia figures into this."

She jerked away from him. "Why *Molilia*?"

"Two reasons: she's Landon's daughter, for one. And for another, she was on a shuttle as the signal first passed through this area. Maybe it affected her somehow. I don't know. Maybe one of the aliens implanted on her through the signal. Maybe that's the face you saw on her when she fell into the pool."

"But...the aliens are after Molilia? That's why they're invading? To get her? Oh no, Sam! We have to stop them! Stop the mission!"

"We can't afford anymore delays." He laughed and reached for her again. "So I've made it my personal assignment to make sure we don't have to worry about you being a security risk."

She pulled away from him. And she'd thought he'd brought her to Rio for another, perhaps romantic, purpose! He didn't care anything at all about her. She was an assignment, that's all. But she pushed that problem from her mind. All that mattered now was Molilia. Greer was determined *not* to let any aliens steal her niece. With or without anyone's help.

# Chapter Twenty-One

THERE WAS MORE TO THE EMISSION NOW, and Walker didn't like it. The interpretation Pereira sent earthside and Walker listened to in Talcott's office had added more to the Tititri message. More, at least, according to Pereira's translation.

*We come. You die next.*

He had little confidence that Pereira knew what she was doing. What made her think she could translate anything without a Rosetta Stone?

Still, H.F. had believed in her. And the possibility of what she'd suggested... A tiny fraction of Walker's mind wondered if an element of truth could possibly exist in Pereira's translation. He recalled the deadly explosions. The failed attempt at SpaceHab. The loss of the Valles Marineris station. The attempt on *Aquarius*. And finally, H.F.

If there'd been no grain of truth, then H.F. had given his life senselessly.

Doubt gnawed at Walker, leaving a bad taste in his mouth.

*We come. You die next.*

H.F. had never really given up his dream of first contact with aliens. The dream had always blinded H.F. to reality. Had his death been the next one, according to the Tititri?

Walker couldn't discount the fact that alien intelligence had once existed. He'd seen the Titan ruins himself, that field of engraved monoliths rising from a sea of methane. Someone had built them.

The universe was a large place, and it wasn't likely — no, make that impossible — that human intelligence co-existed *in the same time frame* with alien intelligence. And even less likely that co-existing intelligent species would ever meet up.

Still...

And then there was that image that Pereira had translated into what might be construed as a humanoid face.

*We come. You die next.*

No, Walker didn't like it. He'd spent the day wrangling long distance with both of them — Jackson, who'd collected the stream of tachyons back at the lab on SpaceHab, and Pereira, who'd interpreted it from the adjustments she'd made to Walker's equipment now aboard the *ISA Centaurus*. Just thinking of others modifying his instruments sent shivers of irritation down Walker's spine. He was tired of getting nowhere. He needed someone to bounce ideas off of, not that he would ever go to Sam Talcott, H.F.'s sham of a replacement. And even if he could talk to him, Talcott was unavailable today. An assistant refused to divulge Talcott's whereabouts, or else plain didn't know.

What if it was true? *We come. You die next.*

What if it was true that aliens were coming? The shamans of the world seemed to think it was true, and they were dying with that knowledge locked up inside them. Were they next on the Tititri's death list, too? If it was true that the Tititri were coming here to Earth, then why should the mission go there?

The turmoil of his doubt was enough to give him heartburn. What would it mean? If they came, and an Earth mission had already left?

No, the translation was wrong. Had to be wrong.

When a call arrived from Van Pelt's lab in the Annex, it confirmed the conclusion Walker had been toying with all along. Van Pelt's assistant had finally gone through the data, retracing Van Pelt's history. Lodged in the trash file were data from the original tachyonic emission, confirming Walker's suspicion that Van Pelt had captured it, too. But Van Pelt had come up with a different meaning. According to Van Pelt, the Tititri weren't messaging "we come."

Instead, they were telling Earth: *Don't come.*

Don't come, don't bother us, godammit, and if you stupid humans don't understand that, then maybe you'll understand a few warning explosions.

*Don't come.*

Van Pelt killed himself because he couldn't handle the truth he thought he'd found. Aliens telling us not to come, to stay the hell away. And mankind pushing ahead anyway, as if the universe belonged to man alone.

At least that was the assistant's interpretation. Whose translation would Walker believe?

He didn't know. He'd been on the job too intensively, and now H.F.'s death and his ex-wife's craziness had infected him with craziness, too. He needed a break. A distraction. Greer, his silly little sister, and Molly with her sloppy kisses.

He was supposed to be hard at work, going over the final checklists with Masambwa, Doc, and Renato in their final day on Earth. But who was going to stop him from walking out? Talcott?

In Talcott's absence, it was easy to walk out.

By the time Walker had crossed the compound to the visitor's quarters, he felt a warm glow in his heart. He rode the lift up to Greer's apartment on the twelfth floor. His unannounced arrival would no doubt interrupt her primping for tonight's farewell dinner.

But when he let himself in, the sitting room stood empty and silent.

"Greer?" he called. No sounds of giggling or baby babble or the patter of running feet responded.

# Chapter Twenty–Two

GREER RETURNED AT DUSK from her disappointing outing with Sam to Corcovado, only to find herself in hell.

Molilia was missing. Hours passed as a blur while a stream of god-knew-who people came and went through the apartment, pawing through Greer's things, claiming the remainder of Molilia's possessions. The *figa*. They took that. Others asked her questions, which Sam tried to field for her. An artist came and sketched out the red-haired, green-eyed woman whose face Greer had seen, superimposed on Molilia's face when the baby fell under the waterfall. Still others trooped through the apartment, vacuuming up samples in their instoanalyzers.

Murmured voices. Muted bells. Doors opening. Closing.

Scalding coffee laced with brandy got her through the darkest hours. Past her own tormented mix of questions. Someone had taken the child while Greer spent the day with Sam.

Ziza.

ISA had checked out Ziza's background. The woman was completely trustworthy. That's what Sam had said. Maybe Sam had set up the whole thing. But if that was so, then Greer had *no* one to trust. God knew, Landon was absolutely useless, sequestered somewhere with his stupid work. Sam wouldn't even let her try to contact him. Wouldn't want to upset the holy mission, after all. Molilia was Greer's responsibility, and Greer had failed.

"What did Ziza want with Molilia?" Greer screamed. "Did Summer hire her? To get Molilia back?"

Sam shook his head and led her aside. "Greer, you're exhausted. You need some rest. Come on, let me help you."

"No, I'm beginning to see things all too clearly." She saw dark circles under his eyes, indicating he was the exhausted one. Not her, not now that she understood a conspiracy was afoot.

"She comes from one of those reclaimed villages in the International Parklands of Amazonas where there are no records on file of genetic background." He looked around, as if for support, or anything to distract Greer from her ravings.

Just then, the door opened again. Sam heaved a sigh and looked away from her. A uniformed officer entered the sitting room and approached the man who seemed to be in charge of the investigation. Through the slit in the door, Greer glimpsed something silvery sparkle out there in the darkened hall.

"Dammit," Sam mumbled. He cast a pleading look in Greer's direction, then followed the officers, gathering in a cluster in the center of the room. From where Greer stood, she couldn't make out what they said from their hushed tones.

She found herself not alone, but unattended. Her breath flowed in easy, little gasps, as if whatever had constricted her up until now was suddenly released. She drank in the charged air of the apartment, as she'd been unable to breathe before. No one was watching her.

That is, no one from inside the sitting room.

But outside, in the dim hall, she saw a flash of red and black. A hand waving at her. A painted fingernail covering crimson lips.

Before Greer had time to think about it, she'd slipped through the slit in the door and stood in the hall. Floor lighting pointed the way to the exit, which seemed more than just the exit of a building. It looked like a way out of the confusion tumbling through her mind. A way, perhaps, to Molilia.

God knew, someone had to do something to find Molilia — she'd be hungry, wet, cold, frightened... No one else seemed to be doing a blasted thing. Sam wouldn't even let her *try* to contact Landon. Not that he would do anything, even if she could reach him.

"Hssst," someone said from the shadows. "I have contacts that could help you find the kid."

She turned and saw the familiar face from holo-vision, only her red and black hair looked more ruffled now than it usually did when she was reporting news of the worlds.

"Why would you want to help me?" Greer whispered. A camera floated somewhere above their heads, but when Greer looked up at it, giving it a distasteful eye, the reporter clicked something in her palm and the bubble drifted down into a pack on the woman's back. "Who are you, really? How did you get in here?"

"Stephia Drummond," the reporter whispered back, ignoring Greer's questions.

"How do you know where Molilia is? Who else do you work for? I mean, besides WNW?"

Stephia shrugged. "I encounter information when I'm working on my stories. And I always get my story. You want the information, or not?" She extended a slim hand decorated with one curving claw, painted in swirling designs of red and black. Its length, as long as the hand itself, rendered that finger useless, Greer thought.

Greer looked back at the crack in the door, through which she'd just left, and considered calling out to the people inside her apartment. That would get rid of the Stephia woman. But it would also send her back inside to her state of helplessness while investigators milled and murmured instead of searching for Molilia. Calling out for help would do nothing for Molilia.

"Going somewhere?" Stephia said. A lop-sided grin worked its way up one cheek, and Greer noticed that the reporter's face was naked. Unpowdered.

Greer nodded, then turned and headed down the hall, following the floor lighting to the exit, the way to Molilia.

"Need a ride?" asked the reporter, on her heels.

For the first time it occurred to Greer that she didn't know how she was going to get there, wherever it was that she needed to go in order to find Molilia. A crashing sound suddenly erupted from the apartment, which was now half the length of the hall behind her. Sam and the investigators must've discovered her missing, Greer thought in a moment of panic.

They'd want to stop her. Stop her from finding Molilia. *Why*? Why had they turned against her? Sam had told her she was a security risk.

Greer's gaze darted up and down the hall. She wouldn't make it to the lift in time. And even if she did, she wouldn't make it down to ground level without being caught. Suddenly, she understood as clearly as if that drowning woman's face she'd seen on Molilia was warning her against ever being caught. Getting caught was a matter of life and death... Molilia's...

"In here," Stephia said, yanking Greer by the wrist and dragging her through a doorway into an old-fashioned escape well. The reporter pulled the door shut behind them, dousing the closet-sized space with darkness.

Greer sucked in her breath. As her eyes adjusted to the dark, she could see Stephia's outline and realized that faint light was seeping in from somewhere. Men shouted in the distance, and feet pounded along the hall on the other side of the door. What would keep them from opening the door at any moment? What would Stephia do if that happened? The way the reporter's body tensed against the door, Greer couldn't be sure what to expect.

Finally, Stephia exhaled and flicked on a wrist light. "This isn't the first time I've had to use the fastest way out of a place," she said with a soft chuckle.

With the faint light of her beam, Greer could see that they stood on a narrow platform encircling the shaft. A smart pole speared the center of the otherwise empty space, and a humid draft whistled up from the well and wrapped around her like a wet curtain.

Stephia lifted her wrist to her lips and whispered into her com. "Tans, honey, we're going to need some help. A little diversion below?" She listened, nodding, then clicked off her com. "Tans is one of the security guards out at the laser fence," she explained to Greer. "He likes his sex very physical — and often. He's well worth the price, at times like these."

Greer wobbled as she inched to the edge of the landing and saw light reflecting off a floor somewhere far below. The bottom of the well, if it had one, disappeared into darkness.

"It's only twelve floors down," Stephia said, leaning toward the pole. "It's clear. Think you can do it?"

Greer swallowed hard and nodded. She was minutes away from being discovered, and for some reason this woman wanted to help her. How much would she charge *her*?

"Follow me." Stephia grabbed the pole and hooked her arms and legs around it. "For god's sake, don't let go. As long as you hold it, it holds onto you."

"Okay," Greer said, shaking only a little bit as she reached across the dead space for the pole. She told herself to keep looking straight ahead, not down into the depths of the well. She used to ride these smart poles as a kid, but never as far as twelve floors. The trick was getting on.

*Careful not to slip before the pole grabs you!*

Greer attached herself, and Stephia told it, "Ground."

Then the pole did all the work, lowering them through the building, floor by floor, slowing as it sensed light, then slipping past. Shadows whooshed up, and the air current ruffled her hair as they dove down, feet first, into dark air. Greer clung so tightly to the pole that her knuckles ached and her palms felt clammy.

She held her breath as they descended the shaft of the building.

# Chapter Twenty—Three

**W**ALKER HAD WASTED NO TIME. He reviewed the House security video, which showed Molly leaving with her babysitter Ziza. He summoned a cart and set it to follow the signal from the chip embedded in Molly. Had Ziza really thought she could get away? Their trail led to strip three, site of the attack on him when he'd arrived here a lifetime ago.

Now he counted out paper money, handing it over to the guard at strip three's laser fence. The security guard who patrolled this section of the laser fence had allowed the power to blink off — how many times before?

Walker figured the guard could be bought to do it again. In exchange for the paper money, which was stacking up in the guard's open palm, the laser would go down for just an instant. Power outages were not uncommon here on the plains of Goiás. This blip lasted long enough for Walker to scramble back into his cart, set to his command, and sail past the boundary usually secured by the laser fence.

This guard apparently didn't mind who bought him.

The cart drove on, following a northwest course across barren plains. No-man's land gave way to shanty communities, and Walker felt sullen eyes upon him as cart snaked on. When he finally came to a river, cart turned due north, following the arrow-straight bank toward jungle ahead, one of the last remaining jungles on Earth, thanks to the Amazon Reclamation project of International Parklands.

The moon glowed from behind a thin band of clouds and touched the river with a streak of rippling light. The water stretched onward to the horizon like an artery that coursed through a sea of shanties as far as he could see.

Walker shivered despite the night heat.

———

GREER LANDED TOO HARD AT THE BOTTOM of the escape pole's shaft, and the thud jarred through her body. Shaking, she took a step backwards, away from the pole. Stephia thrust a canister into Greer's hand.

"Here, spray this repellant on," Stephia said. "You'll need it where we're going."

"Where are we going?"

"Just do as I say if you want to save the kid."

"Oh god!" Her fingers trembled as she sprayed the bitter-smelling mist in a cloud that enveloped her. "What are they going to do to her?"

Sam had betrayed her. All along, she'd thought she could trust him. A romantic outing to Rio, indeed. He'd just wanted to get her away so that his woman — Ziza — could steal Molilia.

Stephia, clearly, *wasn't* one of his women, and so Greer followed her, running to keep up across a barren landscape. The reporter had obviously been this way before. Their trail led to the contact named Tans, who led them to a river, where a man, dark and silent as a shadow, waited for them with a boat. Stephia and the man exchanged urgent whisperings, and then the man pulled Greer on board, a little rougher than necessary, she thought, and shoved her onto a hard, wooden seat.

They drifted past dead, silent buildings. But when she listened closely, they weren't so silent. Water lapped against foundations, drumming out the steady beat of a rhythm. Insects hammered messages across the void. Thank god for her repellant.

But she heard something else besides the insects' mating call. In the distance. Something didn't belong to this landscape abandoned by the human world she knew. Moans?

The whites of Stephia's eyes glittered at her in the moonlight. Sweat glistened on her brow. The fever of a story consumed her. "You hear them? The women? They have what we're both after. I've been waiting for this story a long time. And now it's mine. I'll reveal the truth once and for all, and then WNW can go fuck itself. I'll own *them*."

So, Greer thought. Stephia hadn't risked venturing into the insecurely secured compound of ISA to help *Greer*; it was for the story. And this wasn't just any story — it was a piece of a much larger one. Somehow, Molilia had become a part of it, and Greer was Stephia's entrance ticket to the event.

Greer glanced over her shoulder at Tans, a forlorn figure retreating back along the plains. He was disappearing back to the relative safety at his station inside the compound. He was a thread of reality in this unreal night. Greer felt alone and adrift, at the mercy of the reporter.

Stephia pointed with her claw at the horizon, where the river flowed in the distance. "That's where Molilia is."

"How do you know?"

The reporter laughed. "We have our sources. Are you surprised?"

Greer swallowed hard, wondering again who Stephia really worked for. More than just WNW? "It's not safe out here." She remembered all the shanty towns she and Sam had flown over, just hours ago.

"For thousands of people, it's safer than where they come from," Stephia said.

"What made Sam do it?" Greer blurted out. "I just don't understand. He seemed so *nice*. Why would he go to such an elaborate scheme to help that woman take Molilia? And why doesn't ISA know it was *him* behind it all?"

Red and black hair swirled around as the reporter faced Greer. "You're lovers. You tell me."

"N-no," Greer said quickly, before stopping to think that she didn't want to reveal to this woman the push-pull attraction she'd always felt regarding Sam Talcott.

Now, she saw Stephia's washed-out face darken slightly in the moonlight. She'd heard the resentment in Stephia's voice as she tripped over the word "lovers." Greer had struck a sensitive chord in the other woman, and now she understood. "She's been on my ass," Sam had told her about Stephia, "ever since returning from Jupiter." But it had been more than that. Stephia had pursued Sam, perhaps for more reasons than just the sake of story. By helping Greer, was Stephia getting back at Sam now for having rejected her?

"He's always lied to me," Greer said, hoping to inspire confidence in the reporter. "I've never trusted him entirely."

"You really don't know, do you?" Stephia said, almost in a whisper. She nodded, as if affirming to herself some truth, then glanced once more at the sky. "That soothsayer kid of yours is the key, and — "

"Molilia? She's not!"

"And Talcott has done a damn fine job of keeping me from her. But not good enough. Now I've got you. You're going to get her for me."

Greer's heart pounded. She felt frozen to her seat and shocked into silence. The landscape floated past as the boatman steered them along and Stephia told her story.

"I understood before anyone else," Stephia began. "When my sources described similar events leading up to the deaths of three different soothsayers, unrelated and located in different primitive cultures on Earth, I figured it out right away. An alien force had possessed them."

*Great*, Greer thought. The woman was nuts. And she'd agreed to come here alone with a crazy woman. To a place where no one could rescue her. *Sam, what have you done to me!*

"Of course, it was only a guess," Stephia said. "Talcott knew it all along, though, ever since Jupiter, where he first touched one of the alien's minds — *that's* what he's been lying to you about, honey. He's tried to lead my investigation astray for years."

*Sam is crazy, too!*

Stephia's voice dropped to a whisper, and her body stiffened as she leaned forward. "Hear that?"

Greer listened, too. Above the thrum of insects, above the slapping sounds of the boatman's oar in the water, she thought she heard voices rustling. But it might have been palm fronds whispering in the breeze.

"They've started," Stephia said.

Who's started, and what have they started, Greer wanted to ask, but there was no time for questions of that nature. Somehow, the surreal night was going to lead her to Molilia. She had to believe that, if she could believe nothing else. No one else. Certainly not Sam. But, could she trust the ravings of a crazy woman?

"Anyway," Stephia said, her voice a bit breathless now, "Talcott staged a fake attack on your brother to divert my suspicions to the Savers. That kept me busy for a while, until Tans finally told me about it. Then Talcott got lucky when that other guy researching tachyons — Van Pelt — hung himself. His suicide came at a convenient time for Talcott, who was trying to keep me off the real trail long enough for ISA to get their ship outfitted."

"But, why?" Greer asked. "Why does the mission have to leave so fast?"

"The kid."

Greer sagged with dread. "No!"

"I couldn't believe it either, honey, not at first. That's why I went to Patagonia. It was hard, even for me, but I persuaded one of the guards to let me interview the kid's mother."

"Y-you talked to *Summer*?"

"Keep your voice down." Stephia clamped her hand around Greer's arm and gritted her teeth. "You don't believe me?"

Greer held her breath and felt the reporter's long fingernail tickle her flesh, producing goosebumps. She tried to pull back, but the reporter's grasp remained tight, pinching her arm. "Um, maybe," Greer sputtered. "It's just so hard to believe. That's all I meant." She had to appease this nut case if she was going to live through the night. And rescue Molilia, besides.

Stephia grinned in the moonlight and released her. "We're running out of time. *Their* time is almost up."

Greer shivered in the muggy air. She didn't want to think what might happen to her — and to Molilia — if they ran out of whatever time Stephia meant. She looked up at the sky and wondered if ISA's security forces would attempt an aerial rescue. They must know by now of her escape. Would they track her before this crazy woman...killed her? Or, worse than that, before Ziza ended up killing Molilia?

"Sam seems so strong," Greer said. "So normal. How could he have fooled everyone into thinking he's normal?" *How could he have fooled me?*

Then a new thought occurred to her. Maybe *Stephia* was lying to her! But she was too stupid to lie. Sam had said so himself. Greer didn't believe either of them, but she trusted the reporter even less than she trusted Sam.

Stephia suddenly cocked her head, listening. She laid her clawed finger against her lips as the boat drifted into a swampy area.

The woman was clearly mad, Greer thought. But did she know enough to actually lead Greer to Molilia? Or had Greer been wrong again? Should she have stayed with Sam?

No, Sam and his buddies were only *talking* about finding Molilia, not actually *doing* anything. It was up to Greer to *do* something. The thought of Molilia made it easier for Greer to rely on the help of an insane woman.

Shrubs sprouted up from the water, and as they drifted along, Greer caught the branches, bending them past her face. Then the boat bumped to a stop, and Greer lurched from her seat. The boatman scrambled forward with his paddle and poked around in the water. He shook his head and exchanged whispers with Stephia.

"This is as far as he can take us," Stephia said. "We'll have to walk the rest of the way."

"Swim, more like it," Greer said.

"Don't be fooled. The water's not deep. That's why we can't get through, not even with this boat." Stephia climbed over the edge and slipped into water that came up just past her ankles.

Greer stood still, except for rocking with the boat. She wondered what kind of animals lived in the water, shallow as it might be.

"Come on," Stephia said. "It's not far." She pointed to a low hill rising above the water.

Was that where Molilia was? Okay, Greer could do this. Anything for her niece. Gingerly, she stepped into the water. A mucky coolness sucked at her feet, but at least nothing bit her. Then something brushed against her ankle — a stick, she hoped. She shrieked and sloshed forward, charging past Stephia.

"Hey, shut up!" Stephia clutched at Greer, but Greer twisted away and lunged on.

Greer was breathing hard by the time she crashed out of the water and onto firm land. Branches snagged her shirt and scratched her legs. She plucked them carefully away, untangling herself, when Stephia caught up to her.

"Thanks to that stunt, now every predator knows we're here," Stephia said. "Including the Mundomba."

"The what?"

"An indigenous women's cult, and they have your kid."

"But I thought Ziza took Molilia?"

"Ziza's one of them. She's just following orders. The Mundomba need Ziza to bring the kid to them. They think Molilia is their new leader."

"But she's just a baby! She can't lead anyone. How could she?"

"That's what we're going to find out." Stephia opened the pack on her back, and the silvery bubble of her camera's eye floated out and drifted up toward the jungle canopy. It flickered, as if hesitating, and then moved slowly away. "Come on," Stephia said. "The cam is tracking them. Let's go."

Just then, something else grabbed Greer, something hiding in the bushes. Its power threw her to the muddy ground.

# Chapter Twenty-Four

**W**ALKER FELT A MIXTURE OF RELIEF, anger, and disgust when he realized that the person he'd tackled was his little sister. "Greer!" He squeezed her arm instead of releasing her. "How'd you get here?"

"Landie! What are *you* doing here? You scared me to death. Let me up."

He let go his grip on her, and she scrambled to her feet.

"Where have you *been*?" Greer said with an edge of hysteria to her voice. "Don't you know that Molilia's been stolen? They're going to kill her, if we don't hurry! But no, I guess you wouldn't know anything about that. Not the way they practically lock you up for your *work*. How would you know *any*thing that's going on?"

"Shut up, Greer," Walker said. "No one owns me like that. Now take a deep breath, and then tell me what you're doing here. And why you're with her." He nodded in the direction of that shark of a reporter. Stephia Drummond kept turning up at inconvenient moments.

"Stephia's helping me find her," Greer said, panting, "since no one else is. They tried looking for you, but I didn't think anyone could find you. I guess someone did, huh? How'd you get here so fast, ahead of us?"

"Never mind that," Stephia said, waving something into Walker's line of vision, making him turn to look at her.

Shit. A gun. Old fashioned, but deadly enough, all the same.

"You don't need that," Walker said, trying to make his voice sound as soothing as possible, given the adrenaline pumping through him.

"Quiet," Stephia said, glancing up at her aerial robot. "Let's get going. You first."

Walker moved slowly, feeling the aim of the gun tickle his back. He followed the roving camera, with Greer hugging close to his side. Stephia followed them into deeper underbrush. Twigs snapped underfoot. Branches slapped their faces. Mosquitoes buzzed his ears, and grasses tickled his ankles. The heat of the story propelled Stephia, pushing them forward with her gun, but it was the thought of Molly that kept Walker going.

And what about the mission? He was supposed to be back there at Headquarters now, helping prepare for launch at dawn. The final launch. If he couldn't rescue Molly, then the launch would have to go on without his assistance. His work wasn't worth the sacrifice of his daughter.

A murmur rose from the other side of a small hill. A rectangular shadow loomed in the not-too-far distance. Cloud-filtered moonlight unveiled it as a building, white, at one time. Now it was dark, its walls splotchy. Its windows were holes, like gaping wounds releasing ghosts from more prosperous times. Stephia ran up the side of the rise, then flung herself down amongst reedy grasses to spy on the silent building. She motioned with her gun for Walker and Greer to get down.

Damn, he wished she'd stop waving that gun around. The reporter's nervous motion compelled him to obey, and he fell to his knees beside his sister. Where had Stephia gotten the old piece, anyway? From the Savers, when Stephia tracked down their story? What had she given them in exchange for the gun?

Something croaked steadily, rhythmically, in a nearby bush. The mixture of silky sand and gritty soil still felt warm this late into the night. They crawled up the side of the rise to its crest, then parted the weeds to peer down at the ghostly view at the bottom of the hill, as far away from them as the length of a soccer field. Swamp currents slid in around the edges of silent buildings, as if searching for a way inside. There were three or four buildings down there, but he couldn't tell for sure, since the structures had fallen apart.

Other crumbling foundations laid out in what had once been the gridwork of village roads. It was a village down there, and it lay in ruins, flooded by rising waters. The biggest building still stood more or less intact. Water lapped at the base of a long, narrow porch, looking as if it floated atop the water. The porch, a dry haven in the swamp, ran along what had once been the building's street front.

The current rolled in and washed out, and now Walker saw that the swamp's penetration wasn't the only source of movement. Something also moved on the porch. This village wasn't so abandoned after all, in spite of having drowned.

As water splashed up around chipped support columns, upright figures broke away. The columns hid camouflaged people, he realized. Molly's kidnappers. They must have Molly down there somewhere, although he couldn't spot her. He knew she was nearby. The baby's chip had led him here. The tribal women who must have Molly swayed and danced as if they celebrated something. Or else they were dancing to the death music of the swamp. Now that he spotted them, he could hear them as well. They sang a chant that matched the ripple of water and the insects' rhythm.

———

A GOD-AWFUL STENCH FILLED THE AIR, smelling like a combination of turpentine and the decay of some small animal. "What *is* that?" Greer whispered, wrinkling her nose.

But Stephia wasn't paying enough attention to answer, not even to admonish Greer for breaking their silence. The reporter clicked the control in her palm, guiding the silvery bubble of her camera silently forward, nosing in for a closer view of the scene below. Then she held out her palm so that Greer and her brother could also see the control screen, which showed the camera's view.

Stephia used her claw to click the zoom button, and now faces came into focus. Faces of women. Greer sucked in her breath as she leaned against Landon.

"What?" her brother asked. "Do you recognize them?"

"There she is!" Greer cried. "It's that woman, Ziza! Omigod! She's the one who took Molilia! Hurry! We've got to find her before they do something awful to her!"

Stephia raised her gun. "First, I get my story."

# Chapter Twenty-Five

ZIZA PAUSED AT THE EDGE OF THE SWAMP that surrounded the flooded village. Writhing women uplifted their bare arms, glistening with sweat. A tunnel of arms led the way to the fat priestess wearing Mãe's garland of fish skulls round her throat.

Ziza would do anything for Doctor Inez. Anything, including coming here, bringing the little girl here. She did not know why Doctor Inez spoke to her now from inside Ziza's head. The voice sounded like Doctor Inez, but maybe she was wrong. Her boss could not possibly be Mundomba, which was only for the women of the jungle. It was not for Ziza to know why or how the voices spoke. It was enough that her people wanted the child here. The waiting time was over. Ziza no longer felt afraid to face death. Death was not permanent. Death was only a roadway to something better.

As Ziza drifted through the tunnel of arms, carrying the child, the women fell into line one by one behind her. Their singsong chant "tee-tee-tree" stirred the night prowlers to a background clamor.

Finally Ziza reached the new priestess and set the little girl down before her. Molilia was just a toddler, but she took it all in with wide eyes and not a whimper of protest. She stood like a miniature queen before the priestess, who dropped her massive arms and fell silent. Likewise, did her throng of followers. Insects missed a beat of their background rumba, as if sensing a change in the air. Frenzy slipped away from the women as they waited for a cue. Layers of flesh of the ample priestess began rippling under shuddery waves. Then her eyes rolled back into her head, leaving only the whites exposed in a face, more black than night.

A universal "ahhhhh" rose from the crowd of women, who pressed closer to the edge of their semi-circle. The priestess's mouth opened, and so did Molilia's, as if they were bound together, like puppet to master. Their chests spasmed. They both struggled for breath.

———

GREER GASPED, TOO, AND FOR AN INSTANT she wondered if the Mundomba women's fervor had reached across the swamp and caught her.

"What are they *doing*?" she cried.

"I don't know," Landon said. "But we're about to find out." Her brother stood up from the bushes where they'd been hiding and strode down the hill, toward the water.

"Stop!" Stephia called after him. "You can't go into the middle of that. You'll ruin everything."

"So shoot me," Landon said.

Stephia actually raised her gun and took aim.

"No!" Greer shouted, lunging against the reporter, pushing her to the ground.

The gun fired a loud crack that split the night air. A blanket of dead silence descended over the jungle. Even the frogs stopped croaking. The insects stopped buzzing. The women of the swamp stopped moaning. They looked up toward the hill where Greer wrestled with Stephia.

"Now you've fucked it up good," Stephia said. "I was only trying to help you get the kid back, and now that won't happen."

"You were going to shoot Landon." Greer scanned the silent darkness of the slope between her and the edge of the swamp. "Landon! Are you okay?"

"Shut up," Stephia hissed in her ear.

Greer felt the hard end of the gun press against her back. She tried to go limp, but she was trembling too violently. Her teeth clattered in her head. "Okay! P-please! Don't shoot!"

Alerted, the Mundomba women parted, scattering away from whatever they'd been doing on the columned porch. They streamed away from the buildings and disappeared into the dark of the jungle, and their departure revealed little Molilila, twirling before a white-garbed woman. She wore a necklace of some sort that dangled from her neck when she swayed, oblivious to the chaos that surrounded her.

"The high priestess," Stephia said. "Evangelists, drugged-out street people, shamans, crystal-seekers. Prophets from around the world, all of them. They've been waiting for their new leader, who will save the chosen few. It's doomsday for everyone else."

Stephia made as much sense to Greer as anything else did on this unreal night. "And they think *Molilia* is their leader? Why on earth?"

"Because of who she is."

"Who do they think she is?"

"You don't know?" The reporter snickered.

"Are you so sure you do?"

"Yes, in fact. It's all in the DNA."

"*You* got her report?" As soon as Greer asked the question, she knew the answer. *Sam.* What she didn't know was whether or not Sam had willingly turned over the results or whether Stephia tapped them from him. "What... did the DNA tell you?"

"It's wrong. That kid isn't human. Close, but she's not like the rest of us."

Greer quaked. Her fingers dug into the gritty sand, desperately grasping for a piece of reality, however small. "What are you saying? She's not like us? Then what is she?"

"Isn't it obvious?"

Greer sobbed and crumpled to the ground. "You're wrong! Molilia's not an alien! She's only a baby." Warm and wet tears smeared across her face. Then she sniffled and looked up from her crouching position, as a new thought occurred to her. "How do you know all this? How could you possibly know, unless... You helped Ziza steal her, didn't you? You knew where she could find Molilia. You're in this, too, aren't you? Omigod, are you one of them? What do you want with her? With me?" The level of her voice rose with each question, matching the tide of hysteria and the waves of dizziness overcoming her.

"Shut up," Stephia hissed, "or else they'll get away. This story is too big to lose now."

Greer realized that the reporter would get her story, even at Molilia's expense. Greer had to stop her, and she also had to stop whatever the women of the swamp intended to do, if she was to save Molilia. She turned her attention back to the scene on the reporter's palm screen and hoped she could come up with a plan. She prayed that Landie was safe down there somewhere and not bleeding out from Stephia's bullet.

# Chapter Twenty–Six

WALKER ROLLED DOWN THE HILL as the bullet zinged over his head. Branches lashed at his face, slowing his tumble. He lay there dazed for a while, listening to a far-off rumbling sound. He felt dizzy, and something warm trickled down the side of his cheek. Blood. He wondered if the whirring sound came from inside his head. Something important he had to do.

Molly.

He shook himself and staggered to his feet, plunging on, tripping to the water's edge. Only swamp water separated him from Molly.

Just then, someone crashed down the hill behind him and pummeled into his back, throwing them both into the water. Greer. He hauled her thrashing out of the water, and then Stephia lunged down the hill, too.

"Hold it right there," Stephia said, waving her gun.

The sound of the baby's babbling floated across the swamp and stole attention away from Stephia's gun. Molly danced and twirled beside the priestess, who slumped unconscious on the floor of the porch.

"Teee-teee-treee," Molly said, singing. Her voice sounded wrong. It sounded all grown-up, somehow. Her spinning tilted her sideways. She tripped and dropped to the ground, then curled into a fetal ball beside the priestess and closed her eyes, as if tired and falling asleep all of a sudden.

"Omigod, she's dead!" Greer screamed and leapt to her feet. She darted into the water before Walker or the reporter could stop her.

Walker ran after her, and no one interfered, not even as they sloshed through the retreating tide. The women, these followers of the fish priestess, crept back from their hiding places, closing in on Molly the baby. Greer zig-zagged around them and reached Molly's side a beat ahead of Walker. Kneeling, she lifted the inert baby's head from the cold, cement floor, cradled her in her lap, and smoothed the tangles of fiery hair, sticking to moist cheeks. "C'mon baby," she crooned, stroking her face. "God, no, Molilia, don't die!"

The air felt tight. Women crawled across the porch on their hands and knees toward them, surrounding them, cutting off the possibility of any escape. Their eyes glowed with the fever of whatever had possessed them in the ritual Walker had just witnessed.

Walker glanced from one to another of the advancing women. How many of them were there, anyway? Sweat dripped from the women's faces. Their focus fixed on the two newcomers, and their lips parted slightly. Hungrily, he thought. They reminded him of creepy, crawly things from the swamp. Reptiles, maybe. Who the hell were they? Tititri? They'd come, then, taking over the bodies of the Mundomba women. Walker shivered in spite of the sweat dripping down his sides. Somehow, he didn't think they were human.

Greer drew Molly tighter. "Wake up, honey." She gave his daughter a little shake, but Molly didn't respond.

The women advanced closer, and Walker helped Greer struggle to her feet, lifting Molly with her. The little girl's head, with that red tangle of hair, lolled against Greer's chest.

Greer looked from face to face and finally screamed, "What have you done to her? She's not your leader. She's only a baby!"

Her outburst must have startled the women, for they halted and returned her stares with faces that fell mute. But their surprise only lasted a few seconds, then the women — whatever they were — continued their crawling march toward the center of the porch where Walker and Greer huddled with Molly. Rosy streaks touched the night with a promise of dawn.

Desperate for an idea to save them, *any* idea, Walker slipped his thumb between his index and middle fingers, like the *figa* Pereira had instructed he give his daughter. He remembered how Molly had rejected it. How frightened she'd acted upon seeing it.

Whatever that meant, Walker had no idea, but he held out his fist in the shape of a *figa* to the women, holding it as if it were a torch. One by one, they gasped and shrank back.

Walker turned to Greer, who carried the child. "Let's go," he said.

Then he noticed that Molly's eyes had opened. It wasn't his *figa*-shaped fist that had frightened the women. It was the transformation of his daughter's face. A green light flickered from within her eyes, as green as an underwater garden. A woman's face shone from under the baby's face. "Wait for me," the woman under Molly's flesh said.

Walker felt his skin crawl at the sound, so unnatural, coming from his daughter's lips. All he'd heard from her was baby babble, and hardly that at all, given the little amount of time he'd spent with his daughter. Now a woman spoke from Molly's lips. Some woman was using his Molly to speak to them.

But the Mundomba women — or were they Tititri? — listened. Unresisting, they fell apart from each other like the parting sea.

Walker tried to remain calm as he led Greer and Molly through their midst. Molly was just a child, he told himself. But what had he seen back there on or under her face? Never mind now, they had to move fast, before they lost their advantage, or whatever it was Molly had made the Mundomba women fear. He wanted out of here before this crowd came out of their stupor.

Which they seemed to do as soon as he and Greer hit the water with a splash.

The sky lightened some more, and the air was filled with the slapping sounds of water splashing. The women cried out behind them. He glanced over his shoulder. A few of them leapt into the water after them. It might as well have been molasses that they plodded through.

He grabbed Molly from Greer and studied her face. Molly's baby face had returned again. What else? What had he been thinking back there? "Hurry," he told Greer, and he charged on.

A new sound, a "whump" that he couldn't place, echoed around them. He glanced over his shoulder again, but a surge of the current tugged at him, nearly knocking him off his feet. The women behind them, Ziza at the forefront, closed on them. They cried out in alarm, held their arms over their heads, and stopped. They turned around, then danced out of the water, climbed atop the porch, and scattered inside the building, through the door, through broken windows, streaming away the same way the tide swirled around, seeking passage.

Ziza disappeared into the night. But that didn't matter right now. All that mattered was Molly. Getting her to safety.

Walker struggled, dripping, out of the water and onto shore. Stephia re-treated up the hill, shouting about something. The sky throbbed above, and Walker looked up. A light moved steadily across the rosy sky, bearing down on them. Greer splashed out of the water, and they hurried up the hill. The hovercraft beat them there and extended a ramp. Mario Renato ran down it, with Sam Talcott on his heels, shouting.

Molly stiffened in Walker's arms. "We told you not to come," a woman said in a husky voice that came from Molly's body.

Walker startled, and Molly wriggled from his arms, slipping down to the ground. The green-eyed woman's face shone from within the baby again.

"Interesting," Renato said, halting suddenly.

Talcott nearly bumped into his back. "It's her! The artist sketched her from Greer's description."

"Leave her alone!" Greer cried. "She's just a baby."

"Maybe so," Renato said, "but the Tititri appear to be using her. To the Mundomba she spoke Umi-omega. To us, it's standard English."

"But in the first case," Talcott said, "it was through the priestess, and now it's through the baby."

"Maybe we can talk to her," Renato said. "Find out what the Tititri want. Save us a long trip."

"Hello," Talcott said, cocking his head sideways at Molly. "Are you the same being who also spoke to us through seventeen of our Earth people?"

Molly's baby face came back. The green-eyed woman had disappeared. Walker wished the Tititri woman would leave his daughter alone and go find someone else to implant on, but he feared instead that she'd only gone deeper inside the baby. Molly pushed up onto her feet, sobbed at Talcott, and toddled away from him, down the hill, toward Greer.

"She's getting away," Renato said, lurching after Molly. "We can't let her get away!"

The crack of a gun sounded. Renato jerked, doubled over, and dropped to the ground.

Greer screamed. "Omigod!"

"She told you not to interfere," Stephia Drummond said, still aiming her gun.

Walker lunged, striking down hard on her aiming arm. The gun fell from her hand, and both he and Stephia tumbled to the ground.

Talcott ran to Renato's side. "He's...dead."

Greer screamed again, and Molly bawled.

"For god's sake, Greer," Walker said, sitting atop Stephia, pinning her to the ground, "get my daughter, will you? Before that Mundomba woman steals her again. I know she's out there. Probably watching us. Waiting for her chance."

# Chapter Twenty–Seven

WALKER HATED LEAVING ZIZA BEHIND out there in the jungle. He wanted to haul her ass personally to Patagonia. But there'd been too few hands, and so Ziza escaped. At least Stephia Drummond was safely locked away now in a holding cell back at Headquarters.

The final launch was on hold, too, awaiting Renato's memorial service. With his death, an empty seat had opened up on the mission. But the Tititri woman living inside Walker's daughter had warned them against pursuing the mission.

"We told you not to come," she'd said.

And humans were going, anyway.

H.F. had been right about his aliens. His death was not for nothing, now that Walker understood.

He understood what else he had to do.

"I'm coming with you, Landie," Greer told him as if she could read his mind. And who knew, maybe she could. Walker wasn't going to discount inconsistencies just because he couldn't understand them. Greer was an inconsistency with her face free of its cake of make-up. "You can't take care of a baby by yourself," she said.

Nothing else mattered anymore now that he had Molly back. The mission could be damned, as far as he was concerned.

The morning following their foray into the jungle, he was throwing a change of clothing into a bag, when the door buzzed him. House admitted the visitor before he could snap his bag shut.

"Going somewhere?" Sam Talcott asked.

Walker grunted. "Don't I get a break for my overtime last night?"

"When you come back," Talcott said, "I want you to take Renato's seat."

"You want *me*? On the mission?"

"You bet we do. You and your equipment are too valuable to miss this ride. No one knows how to operate it better than you."

Well. It was about time someone other than H.F. recognized his value. "The Tititri don't want us to go. You have any idea why not?"

Talcott shrugged. "That's for you to find out. You've already talked to them once. Maybe they'll talk to you again. The mission is a go, no matter what they want."

"There's something I've got to do first," said Walker. He wasn't doing anything more until after he took a side trip — with Molly and Greer — to Patagonia. The Tititri had used Summer, too, and it was time to set her free.

"You still work for us, remember?"

"Sure, I remember," Walker said. "I won't be gone long." It was time to let go of old anger and set himself free, too.

# About the Author

While living in Brazil as a teenager, Rebecca S.W. Bates began stargazing with her first reflecting telescope and discovered her awe for Alpha Centauri. Later she became a Spanish teacher and now writes full time and travels as much as possible. Before she started publishing, she won several awards and contests. Her first novel — *The Drowning of Chittenden*, by Rebecca Williamson — was published in 2000. As Rebecca S.W. Bates she has published several science fiction and fantasy short stories, including her story that appeared in the Colorado Book Award finalist anthology *Broken Links, Mended Lives*. Several other short science fiction stories will appear in *Tough Mothers*, an anthology that will be released later this year from D.M. Kreg Publishing. *The Signal* is her first speculative novel and the first book of a trilogy. A readers' discussion guide can be found on her publisher's website at dmkregpublishing.com.

www.ingramcontent.com/pod-product-compliance
Lightning Source LLC
Chambersburg PA
CBHW051919240626

47153CB00004B/1288